A SHORT RIDE TO HELL

When a Wells Fargo stage is robbed and all the passengers murdered, Sheriff Luke Callaghan is suspicious of Jackson Tate's claim that it was the work of Apaches. He sets off in pursuit of Tate and his gang, only to find himself battling the gun-running Mexican bandit Hector Salinas. Things go from bad to worse when Callaghan is forced to defend his beloved town of Maxwell, prove the innocence of his friend, and rescue his sweetheart from a kidnapping.

PAUL GREEN

A SHORT RIDE TO HELL

Complete and Unabridged

LINFORD
Leicester

First published in Great Britain in 2017 by
Robert Hale
an imprint of The Crowood Press
Wiltshire

First Linford Edition
published 2021
by arrangement with
The Crowood Press
Wiltshire

A catalogue record for this book is available
from the British Library.

ISBN 978–1–4448–4592–1

Published by
Ulverscroft Limited
Anstey, Leicestershire

Set by Words & Graphics Ltd.
Anstey, Leicestershire
Printed and bound in Great Britain by
TJ Books Ltd., Padstow, Cornwall

This book is printed on acid-free paper

1

The sun's mad yellow eye cast its burning gaze over the Chihuahua desert as four mounted men sat waiting on top of a canyon. Their leader scanned the arid landscape below as he peered through a telescope.

'It's coming,' he announced before snapping the instrument shut.

His companions stiffened as their mounts stirred and a cloud of dust appeared in the distance below them. The faint sound of galloping hoofs grew louder as the outline of a coach drawn by six horses came in to view. Jackson Tate shoved the telescope back into his saddle-bag and rearranged the folds of the dustcoat he wore to ensure protection of the expensive grey suit beneath.

'Quite the dandy, ain't you Tate?' mocked Seth Fuller, a burly, unshaven

1

individual who cradled a revolving rifle across his chest, 'A guy has to be nuts to wear stuff like that in this heat.'

'Just do your job,' Tate told him without so much as a glance in his companion's direction.

Fuller patted the weapon almost affectionately. 'Don't you worry none. When this baby sings, the crowd don't get to go home no more.' Then he laughed at his own witticism, displaying a row of blackened teeth.

'Are you sure it's the right one?' asked Judd Silver. Tall and fair haired, he sat bolt upright in the saddle and his gloved right hand never strayed far from the ivory-handled revolver sitting snugly in its holster.

'I told you. There's no other stage due here today,' Tate replied before glancing toward the youngest member of the group who sat the furthest to his left.

'Are you ready, Billy?'

The nineteen-year-old responded with a high-pitched giggle as he fitted an arrow into his bow. 'Sure am, and I ain't particular whether it's the right stage or not, ain't particular at all so long as I can finish 'em the way I want.'

Tate nodded curtly. 'Then let's do it.'

The Concord stage from El Paso to Tucson was now almost directly below them, its red paint obscured by a thick layer of dust beneath which even the words *Wells Fargo*, proudly etched in gold lettering, could barely be seen. Billy Gaunt loosed his first arrow and the driver made a gargling noise as his hands dropped the reins and flew up to his throat. Blood gushed from the wound and frothed between his lips as, eyes bulging, he slumped sideways.

The man riding shotgun had no time to decide whether to return fire or take over the reins before Billy's second and third arrows thudded into his chest. As he tumbled to the ground, there were shouts of alarm from inside the vehicle. Men sitting by the windows reached for their weapons, but by this time the Tate gang were riding hard toward them and

Seth Fuller was letting off a volley of well-aimed shots that ripped through the curved wooden body of the coach. Meanwhile, Billy Gaunt leaped nimbly from his saddle on to the front seat and brought the galloping horses to a halt. His companions now surrounded the stage and waited to hear if any sound came from inside.

'Please don't shoot, we're coming out!' cried a male voice. The door creaked open and a young man in a derby hat emerged, leading a young woman by the hand. Four other passengers lay sprawled across the seats inside, blood pooling from their wounds on the floor of the coach. As the young couple stepped over the bodies, an old man slid in front of them with a groan, his hands clawing at the sand as he tried to crawl away, his shirt front soaked with blood. The girl screamed as Judd Silver whipped out his revolver and shot the hapless passenger through the head. Her companion stepped over the body and

4

then placed a protective arm around her as she sobbed with fear.

'We won't give you any trouble, just let us go,' pleaded the young man as his round, dark eyes darted from one man to another.

'You look like a half-breed,' commented Seth Fuller sourly.

'My grandpa was Mexican,' he replied. 'It's not a reason to kill me, is it?'

'I don't see why not. Your woman there looks mighty fine though. I could sure have some fun with her!' chuckled Fuller in response.

'That's enough, we're wasting time!' said Tate abruptly, gesturing with his revolver. 'Go help Billy up there with the treasure box. We'll see about letting you two go when we've got what we came for.'

The youth whispered some words of reassurance to the girl and then scrambled up beside Billy to shoulder some of the box's weight.

Constructed from Ponderosa pine,

oak and iron, it was designed to withstand the rigours of a long journey, but the large padlock was no protection against a determined band of thieves. Once it was on the ground, a single shot from Silver's revolver was all it took for the lid to burst open.

'Well, I'll be damned!' gasped Fuller as the men surveyed its contents including wads of cash and bags with dollar signs on them which obviously contained coins. 'There must be thousands in there!'

'Apaches attacked a cavalry column last month,' explained Tate. 'It was carrying an army payroll to Fort Bowie so they decided to send the next lot by stage. At least that way the money's insured because Wells Fargo always cover their clients' losses.'

'You're one clever bastard, Tate, I'll say that for you,' remarked Silver in admiration.

Billy now leaped down from the driver's seat and noticed the girl. 'Well, look here now. You're worth all the money in that box, darlin'. Why don't you give your sweet little Billy a kiss, huh?' He sidled up to her and ran a grubby hand down her curtain of blond hair. As she flinched in terror, he raised a knife to her throat. 'Hush now, you wouldn't want little old Billy to slit your pretty throat, would yuh?'

'You've got what you came for. Why don't you just let us go?' asked her companion.

'You've seen our faces. That could put a rope around all our necks,' replied Tate.

The blood drained from the youth's slightly sallow complexion. 'We won't tell anyone. We'll just say you all wore masks, won't we Victoria?'

The girl nodded between sobs as Billy continued to hold a knife at her throat. 'Victoria. Now that's a real pretty name. It'll be a shame to have to kill you, it really will.'

Silver pointed toward the gun belt the young man was wearing. 'I tell you what, if you can outdraw me in a fair fight, we'll let you and the girl go. How's that sound?'

'I'm no gunman. I'm just Joe Willis, a lawyer's clerk on my way to Tucson to start a new job. I'm planning to marry Victoria when we get there. That's all I care about, honest.'

'If it was up to me, I'd leave you be,' Silver told him. 'Billy's different though. Apaches killed his whole family when he was seven, and he spent the next seven years being brought up by them. He learned all their ways, including what they do to captive women.'

'OK, I'll fight.' Willis swallowed hard. 'What happens if I don't win?'

'We'll ask young Billy to go easy on your sweetheart, seeing you're so keen to defend her honour,' answered Tate. He jerked his head in Gaunt's direction and the young killer hustled the screaming girl away behind a pile of rocks. This was followed by the sound of her dress being torn and the screams grew louder.

'I wouldn't waste any more time if I were you,' remarked Fuller.

Willis immediately went for his gun. He was surprisingly fast for a clerk who claimed to be inexperienced at handling pistols, so Silver was caught slightly off guard. The gunman's bullet hit the youth squarely in the chest and he slumped forward but managed to let off a shot as his arm was flung sideways. Silver looked down at the crumpled figure lying in the dust and shook his head. 'Well, I'll be damned. I didn't think he was gonna get to fire that thing.'

'That damn conscience of yours gave him the chance,' said Tate.

'Blast you to hell, I killed him, didn't I?'

'You should still have done it quicker,' protested Fuller. His companions noticed that he was leaning over in the saddle and clutching at his stomach. Tate drew the man's jacket aside and noticed the blood seeping between his fingers.

9

'That looks bad.' He handed Fuller a large handkerchief to place over the wound.

'It looks worse than it is. I can still ride,' protested his subordinate, wincing as he tried to staunch the flow of blood.

Tate shook his head, placing his hand on his revolver. 'Not to El Paso you can't.'

Silver consulted a map. 'There's a small town about ten miles east of here, a way station called Maxwell where the stage probably changed horses. There might be a doctor there and Seth could rest up.'

Tate's eyes narrowed. 'The doctor will ask how he got shot and what happens when people find out about the stage?

The sounds of struggle, accompanied by increasingly anguished screams, had continued throughout their conversation.

'God damn it Billy, hurry up and stop torturing that girl!' shouted Silver in exasperation before answering his boss. 'We'll say he got shot when we drove off the Apaches and that we came across 'em attacking the stage but were too late to save anybody.'

Tate nodded his approval. 'They should swallow that, provided Billy does a good enough job here. Besides, it'd be a shame to lose a good man.'

Silver noticed Tate's hand drop back to his side and shook his head in disgust. 'You really thought about finishing him off, didn't you?'

His leader shrugged. 'You can't carry an injured man when you're on the run.'

'Listen, if you choose to ride with a man you should stand by him. Hell, you're just like a hyena otherwise.'

Tate grinned in response. 'Hyenas are pretty smart and they survive, don't they? Besides, I never knew that conscience of yours was quite so tender.' He gestured at the scene of carnage they had created with a sweep of his arm.

Billy Gaunt appeared at that moment,

carrying the dead girl's scalp. 'Can I do the others now?' he asked his leader.

'Sure, go right ahead,' Tate told him. Gaunt immediately set about scalping the other corpses with obvious pleasure while his companions looked away.

'Thanks for standin' up for me,' an ashen-faced Fuller remarked.

'It was nothing,' shrugged Silver. 'Just you rest easy while we sort out the loot.' He and Tate then set about removing the cash from the treasure box and divided it between the four saddle-bags.

'It's too risky to take this into town with us, so we'll have to bury it somewhere,' said Tate.

'Looking at this map, if we head south for a few miles we should pass by the ruins of an old mission. That's as good a place as any. Then we can get back on the road to Maxwell.' Silver turned to his companion. 'Can you hold up that long, Seth?'

'He'll have to,' said Tate as Fuller nodded weakly.

Gaunt had now finished his grue-some work and untied the horses, sending each one off into the desert with a smart smack on the rump. Having removed the bodies to scalp them, he then set alight to the inside of the coach. The men watched as the wooden frame splintered and blackened beneath the flames. The horsehair stuffing inside the upholstered seats added a pungent odour.

'You'll have to get rid of those scalps, Billy. We can't take them where we're going,' Tate told him. The younger man reluctantly tossed them into the flames, muttering that no real Apache would do such a thing. The cavalry had rescued him from his captors at the age of fourteen, but by then the idea of being a warrior had become fixed in his mind. The world of white society had long since lost its appeal, and there was nowhere he truly belonged. He had joined several gangs since escaping from a mission school, but only Tate's offered him a chance to use his peculiar talents and with that a measure of acceptance, though Silver thoroughly despised him.

'Just make sure you behave yourself when we get to the town. We don't want to attract any suspicion,' the gunman warned him, as if reading his thoughts.

'I'll pretend to be one of the heroes you're gonna tell 'em we are,' sniggered the youngster in response.

'I swear to God that kid ain't right in the head,' muttered Fuller, his teeth gritted in pain.

'Come on, let's go. There's no sense hanging around here waiting to get spotted,' Tate commanded them and the four riders picked their way through the desert as buzzards circled overhead, waiting to land on the corpses they left behind.

Maxwell was not much of a town but it was growing. The discovery of an underground spring by a prospector called Max Carver some thirty years before had led to the development of a small settlement dubbed *Max's Well*.

When it finally became clear there was no gold to be had, Carver turned the place into a way station for the rapidly expanding stage network, and shortened its name. Following the old man's death two years ago, his son Matt took over as station agent and innkeeper, ably assisted by his wife Rosie, at just around the time Luke Callaghan was elected the budding town's first sheriff.

Callaghan stood on the veranda outside his office, a building which also contained the small jail, and looked across a dirt road to the row of adobe and wooden buildings on the other side. Arthur Norris stepped back from the freshly painted sign, which declared that Maxwell now had a post office from which you could send and collect mail as well as telegrams.

'It looks good, Arthur,' Callaghan called across to him.

'Yes sir, now we'll really put Maxwell on the map!' The new postmaster stood at only five feet two inches, but his short, stubby legs carried him over to

Callaghan at a surprisingly swift pace. His china-blue eyes blinked behind round, wire-framed spectacles as he continued extolling the virtues of his adopted home and its prospects. 'Soon, Matt and Rosie will have turned that inn of theirs into the swankiest of hotels. This will be the best place to stop for miles around!'

'Aren't you forgetting something? Maxwell's not an overnight stop on the road to Tucson, except for lone travellers not using the stage, and we don't get many of those,' Callaghan reminded him.

'Not yet it isn't, but El Paso's over a hundred miles to the east, Fort Bowie is a hundred miles to the west, and you ride another hundred miles west after that to reach Tucson. Now, can you name me one place between here and there that isn't a flea-infested hell hole?'

'No, I can't,' conceded the sheriff. Perhaps the little man was right. His enthusiasm was certainly infectious.

It was at that moment that four riders emerged out of the heat haze, one bent low over his saddle. Callaghan looped his thumbs into his gun belt.

'Trouble, Sheriff?' enquired Norris.

'I hope not,' murmured Callaghan as he strode towards them.

'Howdy, it looks like you've an injured man there.'

Tate levelled his gaze at the tin star pinned to Callaghan's leather waistcoat before replying. 'Yeah, we had a run-in with some Apaches back there on the road.'

'The stage came through here a while ago. Do you happen to know if . . . ?'

'I'm afraid there's no one left alive, Sheriff.' The dark-haired man in the dustcoat shook his head with a mournful expression — but Callaghan noticed that the look in his still, olive-green eyes did not change beneath their hooded lids.

'We drove 'em off, but they'd just about finished their heathen work. It was too late for us to save anybody,' his fair-haired companion added.

'Well, we'd best get your friend inside the way station and cut that bullet out,' Callaghan told them. Then he turned to Norris who had been standing alongside him. 'I think you'd best send a telegram to Fort Bowie and let the commander know what happened out here.'

'I'll get on to it right away, Sheriff.' The postmaster then scurried back across the street.

Callaghan then led Fuller and his companions to the largest building in the town, an adobe structure with a thatched roof and a stable block at the side. Matt Carver, a barrel-chested former blacksmith who stood at well over six feet, strode over to join them, wiping his hands on his apron.

'There's a man here whose been shot and needs urgent medical attention,' Callaghan told him.

'I'll send Stevie along to get Doc Prentice,' Carver replied as he took Fuller's weight, lifting him down from his horse as if he was no burden at all.

'We're glad to find you've got a doctor,' said Silver.

'Well, he's actually a veterinary surgeon, a horse doctor mainly, but he hasn't killed any of the humans he's treated yet. In fact he even delivered a baby last week, and he's a dab hand at pulling teeth, too.'

'I don't care if he's the devil himself so long as he gets this bullet out,' groaned Fuller as he was carried inside and laid out on a large dining table.

Carver called out to a tousle-haired boy aged about ten. 'Stevie, run along to Doc Prentice and ask him to come here quick. A man's been shot.'

'Yes, Pa.' The boy ran off, and his mother emerged from the kitchen. Rosie Carver was a matronly woman, almost the same size as her husband, but she moved with surprising swiftness to fetch towels and hot water.

'I don't know what the world's coming to when men can't stop shooting each other!' she complained as she removed the bloodstained handkerchief and set about cleaning Fuller's wound.

'It was Apaches, Ma'am,' said Tate.

'The stage was attacked and no one left alive,' added Callaghan.

'I can hardly believe it!' she declared. 'There've been no problems with Apaches since Matt's father first came here. He made peace with them, let them use water from the well. Then they moved away during the war.'

Callaghan nodded slowly. 'I've been thinking the same thing myself. Anyway, Arthur's sending a message to Fort Bowie, so we should have the cavalry here in a few days.'

'Thank God for the telegram!' declared Rosie.

At that moment, a sombre black-suited figure stepped across the threshold carrying a black bag. Prentice removed his hat and jacket and rolled up his sleeves before washing his hands. He peered at the wound over a pair of half-moon spectacles and then addressed the injured man.

'You've lost a lot of blood and will need to rest up a few days. This will hurt some but I'd best do it quickly.' He turned to the others around the table. 'Hold him still please.'

'Hey Doc, how about a shot of whiskey first?' asked Fuller.

'If I waste time getting you drunk you'll be dead,' said Prentice, selecting a long metal instrument that resembled a pair of tongs. The patient was given a piece of wood to bite on as the horse doctor briefly probed the wound, then thrust the implement inside before triumphantly pulling out a bullet.

'Here's the culprit,' he declared. 'It must have been fired from a pistol at close range.' Prentice then expertly stitched the wound and applied a clean bandage. 'All done, you can have that drink now if you want it, but just the one, mind.'

'So, how many of them were there?' asked Callaghan as Prentice left.

Tate shrugged. 'I'm not sure, about a dozen I guess.'

The sheriff frowned in puzzlement. 'Are you saying the four of you got up close enough to be surrounded by those Apaches and survived?'

As Tate hesitated, it was Billy Gaunt who answered with a snort of derision. 'Of course not! A few white men ain't no match for true Apache warriors! We was up on a canyon and Seth fired on 'em with his revolving rifle. It weren't exactly what you'd call a fair fight and they just scattered.'

'It almost sounds like you're on their side,' remarked Matt Carver.

'You'll have to excuse Billy. He has a funny way of expressing himself, but he don't mean anything by it,' said Silver.

'There's just one thing I don't understand,' remarked Callaghan. 'Doc Prentice said the bullet he took out was fired from a pistol at close range, but you say the Apaches were some distance away.'

'Me and Tate were firing pistols as we

rode toward 'em, so maybe Seth got hit by a stray bullet,' suggested Silver.

Tate nodded. 'I guess so, there's your answer, Sheriff.'

'That would explain it,' conceded Callaghan. 'Well, the army will probably have a few questions for you when they come out here to investigate, so I'd appreciate it if you'd stick around until they arrive.'

Tate exchanged a brief look with Silver before he replied. 'We told you what happened, Sheriff. It doesn't seem like there's a whole lot to investigate.'

'Yeah, go out there and look around if you don't believe us,' grumbled Fuller.

'I never said I didn't believe you, but I will go out there. It'd be good to bring those poor folks back here and bury them in our churchyard,' replied Callaghan.

'I'll come with you,' said Carver. 'We'll get the doc and Linus Selby to help too.'

'Do you want us to come along? It

seems like the least we can do,' added Tate in a display of friendliness. 'Don't pay any mind to what Seth just said. He's inclined to get grouchy when he's in pain.'

'Forget it and stay here with your friend, you've done enough already.'

'Rosie will prepare a couple of rooms for you and fix you some food,' added Carver as the two men left.

Once the two men were outside, Callaghan turned to his companion and asked him what he thought.

'I'm not sure, Luke, something doesn't add up. Like Rosie said, my pa made peace with the Apaches around here years ago and we've had no trouble since. Then this sudden attack and what were those men doing out here anyway?'

The sheriff nodded. 'That's what I figured and they seemed pretty cagey too, like they were trying to hide something.'

When they reached Linus Selby's hardware store, a crowd was gathering

and the townspeople quickly surrounded them.

'Is it true, Sheriff? Did them
murderin' savages really attack the
stage and kill all those people?'
demanded one elderly resident.

'What if they come here and attack
the town?' added an anxious young
woman.

'Come on folks, just calm down a
moment. A telegram's been sent to Fort
Bowie and I'm sure the army will
provide men to patrol the area and look
into what's happened. Now I know
there's been trouble with Apaches
elsewhere in the South West but we've
had none here, so let's just wait and
find out the facts before we do anything
else.'

'It'll take days for the cavalry to get
here. We should get a posse together
and find those savages ourselves!'
shouted Mick Harper, Linus Selby's
belligerent young nephew. He worked
in his uncle's store but considered
himself to be quite the fighting man.

Callaghan had put him in jail for the night once for his part in starting a drunken brawl.

'Have you ever fought Apaches, Mick?'

'So what if I haven't?' demanded the younger man with a show of bravado. 'I ain't scared of 'em anyhow!'

'No, you haven't the good sense to be scared,' Callaghan told him. 'Well, I fought Apaches when I was in the army, and let me tell you they damn well terrified me. If an Apache has no horse, he can run almost as fast as a man can ride. He'll keep it up for twenty miles and then fight a battle at the end of it, a battle his side are likely to win because they're the smartest, toughest foe you're ever likely to meet. You're no match for an Apache, Mick, so just leave the fighting to those who can do the job.' Then he shoved the young man aside and strode into the hardware store as the crowd melted away.

'Is that boy giving you trouble again, Sheriff?' asked Linus Selby, the dome of his bald pate glistening above a pair of bushy black eyebrows.

'It's nothing I can't handle. Can you trust him enough to leave him in charge of the store for a few hours?'

'Sure, it'll do him good to be kept busy. What can I do for you?'

'It's not a pleasant job, I'm afraid. Matt's helping me bring back the bodies of those poor murdered folks to give them a decent burial. I'm going to ask Doc Prentice to come along too but we could use your waggon, not to mention your skill as a coffin maker.'

'Consider it done. I'll come with you right away and get them measured up.' Selby untied his apron and called out to his surly nephew.

'Get yourself behind that counter and finish the stock inventory. I'm going out for a while,' he told Mick as the young man shuffled in and obeyed without a murmur of protest.

'You might not be scared of Apaches but your uncle's a different matter, eh

Mick?' joked Carver as the three men left the store.

Doc Prentice readily accepted Callaghan's invitation to go with them, giving a final pat to the sick pinto he had been treating.

'Bring that bullet you took out of Fuller's stomach with you, Doc. It might just come in handy,' the sheriff told him.

Minutes later, Selby hitched up the waggon and the four men set off through the desert. They had gone about ten miles when Callaghan spotted black buzzards in the distance, swooping over the burnt wreckage of the stage. He rose in his seat and shouted at them, waving his arms in the air but they continued their grisly task of feeding on the corpses left to rot in the noonday sun. He then let off a couple of warning shots and they flew off at once. 'We'd best hurry. Those critters will be back soon,' remarked Prentice dourly as Selby drew the waggon to a halt.

The four men jumped down and Prentice began a cursory examination of the bodies. 'It looks like an Apache attack at first glance,' he began. 'They used arrows to kill the driver and the guard. This poor girl was raped and the way they've been scalped . . . ' His voice trailed away and he covered his face with his hands.

Carver peered inside the coach and saw the burned remains of the occupants before he was violently sick. Selby put a comforting arm around his shoulders and handed him a canteen of water. 'You let me handle that part. I've made coffins for all kinds of folks killed in all kinds of ways so my stomach's stronger than most.'

Callaghan's gaze was drawn to the young man lying in a crumpled heap, a Remington clutched in his dead hand. He bent down and prized the gun from the stiffening fingers' embrace. The sheriff sniffed the muzzle and then peered inside the chamber.

'Firing this pistol was the last thing

the poor soul did before he died. Hey, Doc, pass me that bullet, would you?'

Prentice fumbled inside his pocket and drew out the bullet he had removed from Seth Fuller's stomach. Callaghan shoved it inside one of the empty chambers to see if it fitted. Then he compared it closely with one of the other bullets. They were all the same.

'Fuller was shot by this man, there's no doubt about it,' he announced, shoving the Remington in his belt.

At that moment, Selby called him over. 'Look at the bullet holes on the burnt door of this coach. If you look closely, you can just make 'em out. See how close together they are.'

'That kid claimed Fuller used a revolving rifle against the Apaches,' replied Callaghan. 'When you let off a round from one, that's what it looks like.'

'There's no doubt about it, then, is there? Those four men attacked the stage!' Carver had barely recovered from the shock of what he had seen, and this new realization was almost too much to take in.

'That's about the size of it, Matt, so we'd best get these poor folks loaded up and hurry back to town. I want those men under lock and key as soon as possible,' said Callaghan grimly.

2

Back in Maxwell, Jackson Tate was worried. 'I don't like the way that sheriff was questioning us. He's suspicious and smart with it.'

'Yeah, I didn't figure on this town having a post office where you can send a telegram. In a few days, we'll have the army crawling up our asses,' remarked Silver. 'I hope Seth's well enough to ride by then.'

'Never mind him. We can't afford to wait around that long,' said Tate.

'We can't just leave him here!'

Tate brought his face up close to his companion's. 'Do you really mean that? Do you like your buddy so much you're willing to hang alongside him?

Silver swallowed hard and there was an uneasy silence. 'Look, Tate. Maybe we're being too hasty here. If Billy did a good job, we're all in the clear aren't we?'

'Sure I did a good job,' Gaunt cut in. 'I'm one man though, and we couldn't leave no dead Apaches lyin' around to make it look perfect. Maybe once the army gets here and they take a closer look, it won't seem so good for us.'

Tate nodded. 'Billy's right. We thought the only people we'd have to convince were a bunch of hicks who don't like Apaches anyway. This is different.'

'So what do we do?' asked Silver.

'We think up a good excuse and leave here right now. We can say we'll be back in a few days to talk to the army, except we won't of course.'

'Then what about Seth?'

'I can take care of him,' said Billy, examining the blade of his knife.

Silver reached for his gun. 'Goddamn you, I'll blow your head off!'

'Cut it out!' Tate told them both. 'No one's going to do anything to Seth. Is that clear? I don't want a posse on our tails ready to hang us all for murder. Besides, he's not dumb enough to admit to anything so we'll just leave him here.'

'To hang for what we all did,' said Silver.

Tate shrugged. 'If you feel that bad about it you can stay with him. I'm sure me and Billy could make good use of your share.'

At that moment there was a knock on the door before Rosie Carver entered. 'There's some ham and eggs downstairs for you all whenever you're ready.'

'We're much obliged to you Ma'am,' said Tate. 'It'll be just what we need before we have to set off again.'

Rosie frowned in puzzlement. 'I don't understand. Didn't the sheriff ask you to stay here?'

'Oh, don't worry. We'll be back by the time the army arrives. It's just that we were already on our way to visit a friend of ours, an old prospector who has a claim about thirty miles south of here. Unfortunately he's been taken ill and his son's gone out there to take care of him. The message we had is that things don't look too good, and we'd like to make it on time to pay our last respects, if you see what I mean.'

Rosie Carver was a warm-hearted, sympathetic woman, the kind who would cry over a sick cat or dog. 'Oh, how sad! Is there anything I can do?'

'We could use some fresh horses,' Silver told her. 'Is it OK if we leave ours here and pick them up on our return?'

'Of course it is. Now you just have a good feed and I'll get my boy, Stevie, to saddle up those horses for you while you're eating. We'll give you the best we've got and look after your own mounts until you get back.'

The three men exchanged sly grins as soon as the woman's back was turned, and then followed her downstairs.

'I almost forgot. What about your friend, the one who was shot?'

'You don't need to worry about him,' Gaunt told her. 'Seth's fast asleep. I figure he'll sleep for a long time.'

By this time, Callaghan and his companions had finished loading their grim cargo on to the back of the waggon and wrapped the bodies in mail sacks. When they arrived back in Maxwell, the townspeople stopped what they were doing and bowed their heads, and men removed their hats as the waggon passed them, before finally stopping in front of the small Methodist church, constructed from timber and painted white. The Reverend Samuel Endicott stood solemnly on the steps and intoned a few words of prayer.

'We've no undertaker or chapel of rest here, Reverend. Is it all right if we put these poor folks at the back of the church someplace until I get their coffins made?' asked Selby.

'This is God's own house, Linus. I can think of no better place,' the minister told him.

Once the bodies were inside the church Selby drove the waggon back along the street to the way station.

'You'll need backup if you're gonna

arrest those men,' said Carver.

'I haven't had call to fire this in a while, but I'm with you', added Prentice as he checked his revolver. 'God forgive me, but I never would have plucked a bullet out of that murdering bastard if I'd known what I know now.'

'After what I've seen today, you'll get no argument from me on that score. Mind if I tag along too, Luke?'

'I'd appreciate it. Fuller won't be able to give us any trouble but the others may put up a fight.'

Rosie was clearing plates from the table when they strode into the dining room. Her husband asked where their guests were and she explained that three of them had left to visit a dying friend but would return in a few days. 'Mr Fuller will be well enough to travel by then, won't he Doc?' she asked Prentice.

Carver quickly told her what they had found at the scene of the massacre. 'Those men are the worst kind of killer,

Rosie, so it's very important we find out where they've gone.'

The plate she was holding fell from her numbed fingers and broke into several pieces as she realized the full horror of what her guests had done, and the danger she herself had been in. Her husband gently assisted her to sit down.

'Think, Rosie. Did you see which direction they rode off in?'

She shook her head slowly. 'No, but they said their friend was south of here. That's all I can remember.'

'They'll be heading east toward El Paso and the border I should think,' said Callaghan. 'How long ago did they leave?'

'An hour ago, maybe.'

'They've had a head start, but their horses will be tired. Perhaps we can catch them up,' suggested Prentice.

Rosie's hand flew up to her mouth. 'Oh, I'm so sorry. I let them have fresh horses and they left theirs here. What a fool I am!'

'Wait! They must have robbed that stage, and they won't have risked bringing what they stole here, so they must have hidden it someplace,' said Callaghan.

Carver turned from comforting his wife. 'You're right, Luke. Fuller will know where it is. If we can make him talk, and they've had to make a detour, we can cut them off!'

The four men rushed upstairs and burst into the injured man's room, Callaghan in the lead. Fuller awoke with a start and struggled to sit up as Selby drew back the curtains. Light flooded through the open window and the outlaw blinked as his eyes adjusted to it.

'What the hell . . . ' he began.

Callaghan held up the bullet Prentice had removed from Fuller's stomach. 'Recognize this? The man who shot you was on that stage. The game's up now. Your friends have run off so you'd better start talking.'

'That bullet don't prove nothin' and

you ain't got evidence worth a spit!' declared Fuller belligerently.

'The bullet holes in the coach can only have come from a revolving rifle like the one you had in your saddle-bag. There were no dead Apaches, only passengers with your bullets in them. How do you explain that?'

'I never said we killed Apaches. We just chased 'em off.'

Callaghan noted that the man's tone was less certain, and there was fear in his eyes as he looked at each of his accusers in turn. Drawing back the bedclothes, he pressed down hard on Fuller's wound so that the killer screamed in pain.

'Your friends aren't coming back,' Carver told him. 'Your one chance is to help us.'

'Turn state's evidence and maybe you'll go to prison instead of hanging alongside your buddies,' added Prentice.

Callaghan released his grip and Fuller groaned with relief. 'Help us and we'll help you. Where did they hide the money?'

There was just a moment's hesitation before his features broke into a grin. 'So that's it, is it? You want the money for yourselves. Well, you won't get a cent unless it's gonna be share and share alike!'

An exasperated Callaghan rammed the muzzle of his Smith and Weston under Fuller's chin. 'I swear if you don't talk now I'll blow you damned head off right here in this room! One . . . two . . .'

'OK, OK! We buried the loot at that old mission. There's a statue of some saint with birds around him. Dig around by the feet and you'll find it.'

'Saint Francis,' said Selby. 'My late wife was a Catholic,' he added by way of explanation.

Callaghan produced a set of hand-cuffs and manacled Fuller's wrists before hauling him to his feet. 'The first thing I'm going to do is put you in a cell.'

'Hey you can't do that! You promised to help me!' the hapless prisoner yelped as he grimaced with pain.

* * *

Digging up the buried loot in the heat of the afternoon took longer than Tate and his companions expected. The three men were tired from their exertions earlier in the day, having ridden hard since dawn to their rendezvous with the stage.

'We'd best get a move on,' said Tate. 'We're pretty exposed out here.'

Silver leaned on his spade for a moment and swigged water from a canteen. 'There's nobody to see us. What would anyone be doing out here?'

'We're out here so why not someone else?'

'Yeah, I was sure I heard horses when I put my ear to the ground a minute ago,' added Gaunt.

'Aw, c'mon and quit that Apache shit. I'm sick of it,' muttered Silver as he bent down to resume digging. A moment later he struck something and let out a grunt of satisfaction. Reaching down, the gunman pulled a leather saddle-bag out of the sand and held it up.

'Good, the others should be just underneath it. Let's hurry,' Tate urged him.

'Give me a hand with these,' said Silver as he dragged the other bags out from the ground beneath him. Gaunt flung them out of the trench they had dug and the three men climbed out to load them on to their horses.

'Hold it right there!' called Callaghan from behind the remains of what had once been an ornate pillar.

Silver instinctively reached for his gun but a bullet struck the ivory handle before his hand was halfway there. The sound of the shot echoed around the crumbling walls that surrounded them. As the three outlaws looked for a means of escape, each of their four pursuers emerged from a different hiding place, all armed with guns and ready to use them.

Tate reluctantly raised his hands and his two companions followed suit. At Callaghan's command, they slowly unbuckled their gun belts and tossed them on to a pile. Doc Prentice deftly gathered them up but without taking his eyes off the captives.

'There's no need for all this, Sheriff. I'm sure we can come to some arrangement,' said Tate.

'Yeah, nobody would blame you if we happened to get away and there's plenty of cash here to go around,' added Silver.

'Let me guess,' replied Callaghan. 'You're about to suggest a split with equal shares all round. Am I right?'

Tate shrugged. 'Something like that. Those folks back in Maxwell can't be paying you much more than a hundred dollars a month. I bet even a professional man like the doc here gets pretty lean pickings in these parts.'

'You make me sick to my stomach,

Tate. I ought to fill you full of holes right here and now!' Matt Carver could barely control his anger as he stepped forward.

'Easy, Matt. These men will be dealt with by the law,' the sheriff told him. 'I'll shoot the first one who moves, though, so be warned,' he added with a glare in Tate's direction.

Selby uncoiled the length of rope he was carrying and bound each man's hands behind his back.

'How in hell are we supposed to ride like this?' demanded Silver.

'They've got a waggon back there, that's what I must have heard earlier,' said Billy.

'That's right, just up the valley. We'll lead your horses while you three walk in front. The first one to try anything gets a bullet,' Callaghan warned them.

Once the saddle-bags were loaded on to the backs of the horses, the prisoners were marched the short distance to where the waggon stood waiting. To Callaghan's alarm, however, it no longer stood alone. The vehicle was surrounded by a band of Apaches, all armed with rifles and the rifles were pointed at them. Both the captors and their prisoners froze as the man who appeared to be the leader of the group nudged his appaloosa forward. It was a fine animal, standing at over fourteen hands in its mottled white coat. The man riding it had strong features, as if carved out of teak, and he held himself erect in a braided jacket that had once belonged to a colonel in the Mexican army, probably an officer he had killed. Callaghan lowered his revolver and gestured to his companions to do the same.

At that moment, Gaunt stepped forward and spoke to the Apache leader. Neither Callaghan nor his companions understood a word, but the young man's tone was defiant. The Apache replied in a voice that oozed contempt as his followers looked at one another and sniggered.

'It don't look like you've made things

a whole lot better, Billy, maybe even a whole lot worse,' remarked Silver.

'What exactly did you say?' asked Callaghan.

'I told him I was brought up by Apaches to be a warrior and asked if I could join them.'

'It doesn't look like he agreed,' said Callaghan drily as the Apaches gathered around them.

Gaunt swallowed hard. 'He said even his youngest child couldn't be captured and bound by white men.'

The sheriff and his friends quickly found themselves bound and herded on to the waggon alongside Tate and his men. They set off at a steady pace, gradually climbing higher on to a low range, heading east.

'I thought you said the Apaches around here were friendly,' said Tate to Callaghan as they trundled through shrublands of mesquite and creosote bush.

'I haven't seen much of them in recent years but I don't recognize any of these ones. They look different.'

'They're what white men call Mescalero Apaches. You usually see 'em nearer the border or in Mexico,' said Gaunt.

'What are they doing this far out?' asked Tate.

The younger man shrugged. 'How should I know?'

'I thought you were supposed to be the expert, the Apache warrior and all that,' jeered Silver.

'At least he can talk to them. That might turn out to be useful.'

'Useful for who, exactly?' demanded Carver, but Tate did not reply, and the men all lapsed into a morose silence as their journey continued. The waggon was driven along a narrow dirt track that wound upwards, the wheels perilously close to the edge as they reached the top of the range. By late afternoon they had emerged on to a plateau and halted outside a network of caves. Callaghan heard a faint rushing sound, and looked up to see where the mountain stream above them trickled into a waterfall, a rare sight in a desert as arid as this.

Their captors prodded them with rifles and gestured for them to climb down. They were then hustled through the mouth of the largest cave and were greeted by the most unusual sight. The richly furnished interior was brightly lit by candelabras attached to the walls on each side, which had been painted white. Rugs of silk and fur covered the ground beneath their feet, while the chaise longe and ornately carved chairs of Spanish design would not have been out of place in a grand villa or palace. One of the chairs was occupied by a man wearing a plum velvet jacket, ruffled shirt and highly polished leather boots inlaid with gold. As he rose to greet them, Callaghan noticed that he wore gold rings on almost every finger.

'Allow me to introduce myself. I am your host, Don Hector Luis Jimenez Salinas.' He then stepped forward and gave a slight bow, allowing Callaghan to observe him more closely. Salinas had a head of thick black curly hair, matched by a neatly trimmed beard, and appeared to be in his late thirties. When his stunned captors remained silent, he frowned slightly.

'I believe it is customary for guests to introduce themselves also, even in this uncivilized country,' he remarked coldly.

'Is it customary to tie them up?' asked Callaghan.

Salinas smiled briefly, showing a row of white teeth. 'That is a good point, Señor, but I suspect you would not have come had the invitation not been made forcefully, and I have been most anxious to make your acquaintance.'

'Why, what do you want?' demanded Tate.

The Mexican came closer and looked the outlaw straight in the eye. 'Surely that should be obvious to you, should it not? The burnt coach, the men killed by arrows and those scalped passengers were part of an ingenious plan, I think. Unfortunately, my Apache friends found only an empty treasure box at the scene. Now it is time to discover what was in it.'

A group of Apaches then stepped forward and threw down the contents of the saddle-bags they had taken. One of the bags split open and a pile of silver dollars spilled on to the ground.

'Very impressive, Aldo, very impressive indeed,' Salinas told the Apache leader who then leaned forward to whisper in the Mexican's ear. Salinas nodded and then gestured for Gaunt to approach him.

'Aldo tells me you speak his language very well. He thinks you must have fired the arrows and taken those scalps. Is this true?'

'What if it is?' asked the younger man suspiciously.

Salinas gestured to one of the Apaches who quickly cut the outlaw's bonds. 'I could use a white man who possesses such rare talents.' Gaunt hesitated for a moment, taking a sidelong glance at Tate.

'Loyalty is a precious thing, my friend, but one can take it too far. I am sure you would not wish to share the fate my associates reserve for their white enemies, no?'

'So long Tate,' muttered Gaunt as he moved over to stand beside his new boss.

'Just what is it you intend to do with us?' asked Silver, unable to hide the tremor in his voice.

Salinas placed a hand over his heart in a mock gesture of sadness. 'It is a matter of sincere regret to me that I cannot find suitable employment for you all, but I bear a heavy burden of responsibility with many mouths to feed. Gentlemen, I am left with no other choice but to leave you at the mercy of my Apache friends who will deal with you as their traditions and their consciences dictate.'

At that moment, having somehow wriggled free of his bonds, Linus Selby lurched forward, his hands extended in a bid to seize their tormentor by the throat. It was a brave but futile gesture and a knife struck him through the heart before he had gone more than a few paces. He crumpled to the floor like a broken puppet without uttering a sound. Billy Gaunt then withdrew his weapon, wiped the blade on the dead man's shirt and put the knife back in its hiding place inside the top of his boot.

'I pride myself on being a good judge of character,' remarked Salinas with a nod of thanks in his new recruit's direction as two Apaches dragged Selby's body away.

'God damn you Salinas, you won't get away with this!' shouted Callaghan. 'You haven't just killed a bandit, that man was a law-biding citizen. Look at those mailbags. Any fool can see you've taken an army payroll at a time when the whole South West is under military control.'

The Mexican smiled as he delivered his reply. 'I think General Sheridan is more than happy to turn a blind eye to my activities. Before I hand you over to my friends, I wish to show you something. Come!' Then he turned to his Apache subordinates and signalled for them to bring the captives forward. They then followed Salinas to the back of the cave where a series of crates stood stacked up against the wall. He picked up a crowbar and wrenched one of them open. It was packed with rifles.

'These are destined for the soldiers of Benito Juarez, rebels against the Emperor Maximilian. That is a cause much beloved by General Sheridan and even the President himself, I understand.'

'I wouldn't have put you down as a revolutionary,' remarked Callaghan.

'Well, the Emperor is running short of funds and has become an unreliable customer, especially since the French withdrew their troops. Besides, the rebels pay more. So, you see, gentlemen, hanging me is unlikely to be high on the General's list of priorities.' Salinas then picked up one of the rifles and stroked its barrel almost lovingly. 'The Henry rifle is superior to your standard carbine with greater firepower. I also have some of those new rifles that came out last year, Winchesters, which are even better.'

'I see you are playing with your toys again, Hector.' All heads turned to look at the young woman who now stepped out of the shadows of the cave. She was dressed in a tightly fitted blue riding outfit that accentuated the generous curves of her tall figure. Her full lips were set in a firm line that indicated disapproval as she glanced at the prisoners. 'Why are these men bound?' she demanded.

Salinas waved a dismissive hand in her direction. 'It is not your concern, Christina. Besides, they will soon be gone from here.'

She responded with a flood of invective in Spanish, which clearly had no effect on Salinas as he merely shrugged and muttered an oath under his breath. Enraged by this, Christina raised the riding crop she held in her gloved right hand and struck out at him. Salinas was a man of quick reflexes and he seized her wrist, holding it in an iron grip until the girl cried out, dropping her intended weapon to the ground.

'My sister has a temper, as you can see. I shall have to redouble my efforts to find her a suitable husband,' the Mexican told his prisoners, although the remark was obviously intended to goad her.

Christina removed the small hat she wore and unpinned the waves of jet black hair piled beneath it. 'Never will I marry any man associated with your evil work. I'll die first!'

'That can always be arranged, dear sister,' Salinas told her with a sly smile. He glanced at his Apache confederate as he continued. 'Perhaps I should just give you to Aldo. I have seen how he looks at you with that hunger in his eyes, a hunger that can only be satisfied in one way.'

The woman gave an involuntary shudder. 'You wouldn't dare,' but her tone was uncertain.

Salinas briefly caressed her aristocratic features. 'Perhaps not, but don't push me too far or you may find me a less than loving brother.'

Christina turned her attention to Callaghan and the other captives. Her almond eyes widened in surprise when she saw the tin star pinned to his chest. 'I see you are a man of the law, Senor. How do you come to be here?'

'I was about to arrest Jackson Tate and Judd Silver over there along with Billy Gaunt when Aldo's men captured me and my friends.'

'Why were you going to arrest them?'

'They robbed a stage and killed a whole bunch of people.'

'Hector, can't you just let these people go? They've done you no harm, after all.' Christina looked pleadingly at her brother.

'Don't be foolish! How long would this hideout remain secret if I did that?

Besides, they are Aldo's prisoners and he has the right to do with them as he pleases. That's always been our arrangement.'

She looked pleadingly for a moment at the Apache leader, but the look in his eyes told him what she would have to do even to have a hope of changing his intentions. Christina squeezed Callaghan's arm and then briefly gripped his bound hands. 'I am truly sorry, Senor, but I have done all I can. Please tell me your name so that I will know whose soul I must pray for.'

'I'm Luke Callaghan, Miss, though I reckon your brother's soul may be more in need of prayer than mine.'

'May your noble sentiments accompany you to the grave,' said Salinas with a mocking gesture of farewell.

Callaghan and his two remaining companions were now hustled out of the cave by Aldo and his men. As they did so, Tate shouted back at the Mexican. 'Kill me and you'll never find the rest of the money, Salinas, never!'

Salinas held up his hand for a moment and the Apaches stopped in their tracks. 'What are you talking about?'

'I never hide all my loot in one place at once, and this time there was a big haul. I split it but you won't get the rest unless you make a deal.'

The bandit stared hard at him for a moment, and then burst out laughing. 'That was a nice try, but you'll have to do much better.'

Moments later, they were back outside in the harsh glare of sunlight. The Apaches mounted their horses but the prisoners were made to walk, trudging down from the range until they reached the endless expanse of desert sand. Their captors kept them walking for several miles and then suddenly stopped. The four men were then made to lie down, arms and legs spread wide while stakes were driven into the ground, their wrists and ankles bound separately to each one. Aldo himself tied Callaghan, grinning as he reached inside the sheriff's sleeve to pull out the penknife Christina had furtively passed to him earlier. He then tossed it a few inches away where it lay just outside the lawman's each.

'Darkness comes soon. Tonight, you freeze, then sun will rise and tomorrow you burn. All of you dead by end of tomorrow, but meantime you suffer as white men make Apaches suffer.' It was the first time they had heard Aldo speak English and his words, chilling in their simplicity, made it clear that a lingering, unpleasant death awaited each of them. The Apaches then mounted their horses and rode away.

None of them spoke, each man thinking of his own fate. Doc Prentice lay next to Callaghan. He let out a groan and the sheriff turned to see that his friend's face was flushed and sweating.

'Take it easy Doc, you've got plenty of time to die.'

'I need one of my pills. They're for my heart . . . God damn it!' The horse doctor gasped with pain. 'My chest . . . It's never hurt this bad until now.' He groaned once more and his breathing started to come in short, shallow bursts.

'Save your strength, don't try to talk,' Callaghan urged him.

Carver lay to the left of Prentice. 'Try not to worry, maybe we'll get lucky and somebody will come by. Hang in there, Doc.'

Prentice did not respond. His breathing became more irregular, his eyes closed and he lapsed into unconsciousness. Moments later, he stopped breathing altogether.

3

'That was a quick end for him, lucky bastard!' observed Tate bitterly.

'Show some decency! That guy never did anyone any harm, unlike us, and he didn't deserve what happened to him,' protested Silver.

'Nobody gets what they deserve. The world's not fair and never has been. Besides, you've done your share to keep it that way, same as me,' Tate reminded him.

'What's the matter with you? You're gonna die, and you've probably got worse things to answer for than even I have. Don't you feel any shame?'

'It's a little late to start having a conscience now,' complained Carver in the absence of any reply from Tate.

'I guess you're right, but a man gets to thinking when he's in this situation,' conceded Silver. Then he called out to

Callaghan. 'I've done a lot of killing, I got used to it in the war, but if I'd been in charge Billy wouldn't have done what he did to that girl.'

'That's easy to say now, but you robbed and killed with that kid, you followed Tate, and you can't separate yourself from any of it,' replied the sheriff.

No one spoke then, and dusk came with a smouldering orange glow as a cool wind blew across the desert. Night fell and inky blackness descended, the stars were tiny pinpricks of light amid a waning half-moon. The temperature plummeted and each man lay shivering in the dark without a blanket, by now feeling the pangs of both hunger and thirst. By noon tomorrow, the thirst would be unbearable and Callaghan hoped he would not last too long. He began to envy Prentice, and felt a pang of guilt at responding to his friend's death in this way.

Dawn came at last, its rose tinted glow a surprisingly cheerful sight despite their predicament. As the sun climbed higher, they heard a horseman approaching. Callaghan lifted his head and strained his eyes to spot the rider. He noticed that whoever it was led a second horse behind him. The three survivors called out weakly, fearful that the man might not see them and ride past. The hoofs slowed to a halt, the rider dismounted and stood over them, blocking out the sun.

'Well, good morning gentlemen. I hope you have passed a comfortable night,' said Salinas sarcastically. He pointed a Winchester at Tate.

'What do you want?' the outlaw asked him.

'Billy assures me that your story about hidden loot is untrue, but it occurred to me that he could just be waiting for an opportunity to collect it himself.'

'That kid has more guile than a barrel full of snakes. You were right not to trust him.'

Salinas smiled. 'Just as I am right not

to trust you.' He produced a sword from his saddle-bag and cut Tate's bonds while keeping the Winchester pointed at the outlaw's chest. Tate slowly stumbled to his feet, weakened from his night of privation. The Mexican tossed him a canteen and he drank from it greedily.

'Your life in exchange for the money. Do we have a deal?'

Tate nodded. 'I see you left your friends behind.'

Salinas patted his rifle. 'I don't want to share everything with Aldo and his men, but don't get any ideas. I'll shoot you at the first sign of trouble.'

'You're wasting your time with this crap,' Silver told him. 'There's no hidden money and the bastard will try to jump you the first chance he gets.'

'Why should you care if Salinas gets what's coming to him?' asked Carver.

'I just don't like seeing him get away.'

'He won't get far once Salinas realizes there's no money,' added Callaghan.

'Pay no attention to them,' Tate told his Mexican captor. 'They're just sore at being left behind.'

Salinas gestured for his prisoner to mount up and ride in front. 'Don't forget, I'll be watching you every step of the way,' he warned. The two men then set off across the desert without a backward glance at those they had left to die.

Callaghan and his companions were not left alone for long, however. Presently, they heard what sounded like a waggon approaching. The three men looked up and the sheriff squinted in the harsh glare of sunlight. It looked like the vehicle was being driven by a woman.

Suddenly the waggon came to a halt. The driver jumped down and Christina was beside him, cutting his bonds with a knife. She quickly freed Carver, then crossed herself when she found that Prentice was dead.

'He died quite quickly. It was his heart,' Callaghan told her.

Christina then turned her attention to Silver. 'What about this one? I know he is a thief and a murderer but we can't just leave him out here to die.'

'I'll take him back to Maxwell as my prisoner and he can sit in a cell with his friend Fuller until the cavalry comes,' Callaghan cut the gunman free and hauled him to his feet. Christina tossed over a pair of handcuffs and he clamped them around Silver's wrists before hustling him on to the back of the waggon. He saw then that she had brought the saddle-bags full of stolen money, some food and water, several Winchesters and plenty of bullets.

'There is time to bury your friend but we must hurry,' Christina said. 'Hector gave Aldo and his men bottles of whiskey last night as a reward and they are sleeping it off but they'll come after us when they wake to find the money gone.'

'What about your brother?'

The girl shrugged. 'I watched him leave at dawn and I knew what was on his mind. Was Tate telling the truth?'

Callaghan shook his head. 'Hector's just blinded by greed.'

'Then he'll kill Tate and head back to the hideout. He'll be after us too, once he finds out what's happened.'

'Don't underestimate Tate, he's smarter than Benjamin Franklin and meaner than a polecat. Salinas might be in for a big surprise,' warned Silver.

Callaghan did not reply but picked up a spade from the back of the waggon and began to dig a grave for Prentice.

'It'll be quicker if you let me help,' suggested the gunman.

'I may not be as smart as Tate but there's no way I'm giving you something to use as a weapon. Besides, you're not fit to help bury a decent man like him.'

'I guess I'm not exactly one of the good guys. Call it an act of atonement if you want. The girl can keep a rifle pointed at me in case you're worried. Besides, we're in a hurry and I'd rather take my chances with the hangman than those Apaches.'

Callaghan exchanged looks with Christina and she nodded. He tossed Silver a spade and gave him a curt nod. 'OK but those handcuffs stay on.'

As their prisoner began to dig, Christina pointed the muzzle of her Winchester just inches from his chest. 'I can't miss at this range and these eyes see everything.'

Meanwhile, several miles away, Salinas was growing impatient. 'You haven't told me exactly where we are going, Gringo.'

'Do you have a map?'

'I thought you knew where you were taking me!'

'Look, just relax. I know it's around here someplace but it'll be easier to find again if I have a map.'

The Mexican felt inside his jacket for the map he always carried with him for the desert was a dangerous place in which to get lost. He handed it over cautiously, without lowering his eyes or his gun.

Tate made a great show of studying it carefully. At last, he found what he was looking for. 'See, here it is. The old silver mine was abandoned long ago and nobody goes there. I figured it'd be the last place anyone would look.'

The Mexican's eyes narrowed into a glare of suspicion. 'You never mentioned anything about an old mine before.'

The outlaw shrugged. 'You didn't ask for any details, just the money. Follow me and I'll take you right to it.'

The fact that they were already heading in the general direction of the mine and it was not far away allayed the Mexican's suspicions slightly, but he remained vigilant for signs of betrayal. Meanwhile, Tate's mind worked furiously to find a way out of his predicament while maintaining an outward show of nonchalance. Salinas had given him some bread and dried biscuits to eat so hunger no longer gnawed at him, but he was still weak from his ordeal. His captor would have to be caught off guard if he was to stand any chance of escaping.

At last they approached the tunnel that led into what had once been a thriving silver mine, though the last seam had been picked clean years before.

'I haven't brought any lamps. How are you going to find it?' demanded Salinas.

'I never said it was inside the tunnel, did I? That'd be stupid. The damn thing could collapse anytime. No, I dug a hole just here, near the entrance.' Tate pointed to where a large stone slab lay and heaved it aside. 'How about letting me have some more water and a rest before I start? The hole's quite deep.'

Salinas felt his pulse quicken with excitement. He had had his doubts but the gringo seemed very definite. Using a large slab to mark the spot and choosing a prominent place with a landmark where no one would expect to find anything of worth was exactly what you would do if you were a

71

cunning thief hiding buried loot. He tossed over the canteen and dismounted, keeping his rifle pointed at Tate while the outlaw drank. After about ten minutes, he waved the Winchester impatiently and tossed over a spade with his free hand.

'You've had enough rest, gringo. Now you dig.'

Tate paced himself to conserve his strength but he kept going until he had managed to dig a slit trench that was above waist height. Salinas was growing more impatient, urging him on with threats and curses.

'I'm going as fast as I can. I was staked out all night, thanks to you,' grumbled the outlaw in reply, feigning a greater weariness than he actually felt. At last his spade struck something, as he hoped it would, for all sorts of debris lies buried in long-abandoned places where men have lived and worked. Tate sank to his knees and pretended that the old sack of clothes he had found weighed more than he could lift in his weakened state.

'God damn it, this gold's heavy,' he protested as he stood aside from the half-buried sack and leaned on his spade.

Salinas peered over the edge of the trench to see that a bag had been uncovered. Excitement overcame his natural caution, and he jumped down to examine it more closely. By the time the first flicker of realization that he had been duped entered his brain, the spade was being swung heavily towards his head and crashed into the back of his skull. The Mexican was stunned, but conscious enough to stagger around and face his adversary. His numbed finger struggled to find the trigger on the Winchester as tears of pain blurred his vision. Tate thrust forward and buried the edge of the spade deep in the bandit's throat, twisting it so it went in even further. Salinas fell back with blood spurting from his carotid artery, and then slumped to the ground.

Tate bent down over the dead man's body and searched his clothes. He found a wallet containing a roll of banknotes and a gold watch. Salinas also wore a gun belt, which the outlaw removed, and he then picked up the Winchester as he climbed out of the trench. His elation vanished however, when he found himself surrounded by Aldo and the other Apaches. Gaunt was with them, and he jumped down from the pinto he was riding before peering over the edge of the trench. He gave a low whistle when he saw the Mexican's body.

'He fixed your boss,' Gaunt told Aldo.

The Apache leader pointed at Tate. 'Where is the money?'

The outlaw looked nonplussed. 'There isn't any. It was just a story I told Salinas to get away.'

Gaunt shook his head. 'He means the loot from the stage. It's gone and so has the girl.'

'Then she took it all by herself,' Tate

told Aldo. 'Did she take the waggon too?'

It was Gaunt who answered him. 'Yeah, plus some guns and supplies.'

'She must have freed Callaghan and the others. I know where they've gone and I can help you find them.' Tate looked pleadingly at Aldo but the Apache shook his head and pointed at Gaunt.

'This one who calls himself a warrior can tell me as much. You die, same as before.'

Gaunt drew his knife and ran the blade under the outlaw's chin. 'If you're lucky, Aldo might let me do it quick, seein' as you've been so helpful an all.'

Tate swallowed hard but then an idea occurred to him. 'Salinas is dead and you need somebody to get those guns across the border and sell them,' he declared, meeting Aldo's gaze.

'I will sell guns. White men think Apaches foolish, but we are wise.'

'I'm not saying you're stupid and you can steal the guns easy enough, but you know as well as I do that Mexican officers will try to cheat you on the price,' insisted the outlaw. Seeing the Apache hesitate, he pressed home his advantage. 'A white man knows the value of money and can pretend to be acting on behalf of the US government. Juarez needs American support and his officers will listen to me, but not to you.'

Aldo considered this for a moment. 'You promise much. What do you ask in return?'

'Let's say ten per cent of everything you make on the sale of your guns. There's also the question of the money the girl stole. After all, I stole it first, didn't I?'

Aldo responded with a wry smile. 'Yes, you white men are good at stealing. Very well, I give you ten per cent of that also when we get it back. Now, come!' The Apaches turned their horses around without waiting for him and began to ride away.

Gaunt removed his knife from Tate's

throat. 'Nice work, I swear you got more damned lives than a cat. I hope you ain't got hard feelings about me being about to kill you just then.'

'You were just doing what I taught you to. I was worried though. A lot of these Apaches like to trade for goods instead of being paid in cash.'

'Not Aldo,' said Gaunt as the two men mounted up. 'He wants a hacienda and a real Mexican lady with Spanish blood, like Christina. He thinks wearin' that colonel's uniform makes him look the part instead of just a dumb asshole.'

The two men laughed as they rode behind the Apaches in a cloud of dust. Soon they would reach Maxwell and catch up with Callaghan. Tate was looking forward to his revenge on the sheriff who had cost him time, trouble, and above all, money. After that he could concentrate on getting his loot back and making his escape from Aldo.

★ ★ ★

Meanwhile Christina drove the waggon at a steady pace as Callaghan and Carver kept an anxious look out for any pursuit.

'It looks like we're safe for now,' remarked Carver as they came within a few miles of Maxwell.

'They'll find us soon enough,' replied Callaghan. 'An Apache can track a man for a hundred miles or more and not lose the trail.'

'You seem to know a lot about them,' said Christina.

'I fought them often enough when I was an army officer.'

'So which side did you choose during the civil war?'

'I didn't. The sight of my country tearing itself apart, men who were fellow citizens killing each other, some of them even members of the same family was too much for me. I resigned my commission just before it started and came out here.'

'That was a brave thing to do,' she told him.

Callaghan shook his head. 'A lot of folks wouldn't agree with you. I've been called a coward more times than I can count.'

Christina snorted derisively. 'They don't know the meaning of the word. You made a stand for peace, for settling things without violence, and that takes courage, just as it took courage to come after Tate and his men.'

'You're right,' agreed Carver. 'I fought for the South and I saw a lot of good men die and killed a lot of good men on the other side too. Then I came back to Maxwell two years ago when the war ended and my pa died. I wish I'd never left in the first place.'

Silver had been listening to their conversation. 'Yeah, that's when I learned to kill. I burned and looted my way through the South with the Union army. When I came out, I didn't know any other way to live.'

'Don't make excuses for yourself,' Callaghan admonished him. 'A lot of men did things during the war they're not proud of but they still managed to put their guns down afterwards.'

The gunman shrugged in response. 'I wasn't trying to excuse myself, just telling you the way it was with me. I killed so many people, civilians some of them, that after a while it stopped mattering.'

They reached Maxwell shortly after that and the waggon drew to a halt outside the way station. Rosie Carver ran outside to greet them.

'Oh Matt, thank God!' she cried as she flung her arms around her husband. 'I was so afraid you were dead!'

'Well, it's really this young lady you should be thanking. If it wasn't for her, we'd all be feeding the vultures by now.' Carver then introduced Christina.

'Well I'm much obliged to you,' she added gratefully. Rosie then looked around at the others. 'Where are Linus and Doc Prentice?'

Carver put his hands on his wife's shoulders. 'Linus died trying to save the rest of us and Doc had a heart attack.'

'There's not much time for explanations or for mourning the dead, I'm afraid,' said Callaghan. 'Apaches are going to attack soon and we must prepare our defences.'

A crowd was now gathering around the waggon and a murmur of fear ran through it. The sheriff stood up and urged them to be calm. 'Now listen to me. We need to build a wall around this town, shoulder high. Use bags of sand, furniture, upturned waggons and anything else you can find that will make a good barrier. Everyone over fourteen must carry a rifle.

'Does that include the women too?' Bertha Endicott, the minister's wife asked.

Callaghan nodded. 'If they can shoot, then yes. We need all the help we can get.'

'What if the Apaches get over the wall?'

'They might, so we'll need folks posted along the street and in buildings to shoot them down if they break through, but most of our firepower should be concentrated along the wall at first. Then, if they overpower us there, we'll just have to retreat.'

'We can build some redoubts further back. I've got some timber we can use,' suggested one man.

Callaghan gave him a nod of approval. 'Good idea, I'll leave that to you. OK, let's get to work. Remember, the army should be here in a couple of days if we can just hold out that long.'

Arthur Norris waved a telegram in the air. 'I had a reply to the one I sent. There's a cavalry troop on way but they won't be expecting to find the town under siege.'

'That can't be helped,' replied Callaghan as he climbed down from the waggon, pushing Silver in front of him.

'I'm no good to you locked up, Sheriff. Why don't you let me help?'

'Because the folks in this town will tear you to pieces if I let you among them. You'll be much safer in jail for now. If the Apaches break through our defences, I'll let you and Fuller have guns so you can defend yourselves.'

Seth Fuller was surprised to see his old friend join him in his cell. 'I thought you'd high-tailed it to Mexico and left me to carry the can.'

'Just wait until you hear the good part,' said Callaghan as he locked both men in before leaving the jail.

'What in damnation's goin' on here?'

The outlaw then listened attentively as Silver recounted the story of his recent adventures, culminating in the news that a band of renegade Mescalero Apaches would soon be approaching the town.

Fuller stood up in panic. 'God damn it, we gotta get outta here!'

Silver shrugged in response. 'What difference does it make? We're gonna be hanged anyway.'

'What them Apaches do is a whole lot worse, we can be sure o' that,' his companion replied.

'The sheriff said he'd let us have guns

when the time came. We can save a bullet for ourselves if we have to.'

'Well, that's a mighty comfort, I must say,' snorted Fuller in derision. He rubbed his stubbly chin as he paced the cell, deep in thought. 'No, we have to find a way to use this to our advantage, Judd. These folks are all scared as jackrabbits right now, and they won't be worryin' too much about us. Maybe there's some way we can skedaddle outta this place while they're all waitin' for the Apaches to come skin 'em alive.'

Silver leaned back in his bunk and rested his head against the wall. 'Yeah, you just think about that, Seth. I don't reckon it'll do either of us any good but go right ahead.'

Fuller gripped the bars of the cell's window, which looked out on to the street. Amid the bustle of townspeople preparing to defend themselves he noticed the bags of cash from the stagecoach robbery being carried into the post office. 'Well I'll be damned,' he murmured as he turned back to Silver.

'What is it?' asked the gunman as he tipped his hat over his eyes for a doze.

'They're puttin' our money in that post office. I guess it's the most secure place, since this so-called town don't even have a bank to rob.'

'So what?'

'What's got into you, Judd? Our money's just there across the street and you're sayin' you don't give a damn!'

Silver raised himself up on to one elbow. 'It was never our money in the first place, Seth. Besides, we got no chance of getting our hands on it.'

Fuller shook his head. 'I ain't about to give up so easy, so just you be ready to move when the time comes.'

The gunman did not reply but lay back down again. There would be no opportunity to sleep once the attack started and he wanted to get some rest while he still could.

Meanwhile, Aldo and his band of Mescalero Apaches were rapidly approaching the town. The alliance with Jackson Tate and Billy Gaunt was an uneasy one, since Aldo distrusted Tate and was not sure what to make of the younger man.

'I can't wait to get my hands on them womenfolk,' said Gaunt. 'Maybe we could take some prisoner and keep 'em awhile.'

'Just concentrate on the job in hand and you can have all the women you want when we get to Mexico,' Tate told him.

'Hell Jackson, you sure ain't much fun sometimes!' protested his companion. 'I gotta scalp a whole lotta men, get drenched in their blood and have my way with their wives before I feel I've fought like an Apache!'

Aldo shot the youth a look of contempt. 'You will never be a true Apache, white boy! The Apache fight for survival, to get what we need. We make our enemies afraid so we can defeat them, but we are not cruel without purpose. We do not lust for their blood or their women. You have learned some of our ways but you do not have our spirit in here,' he declared, striking his breast to emphasize the point.

'Just wait until you see the kid fight,' Tate told him. 'Apache or not, Billy will do his part.'

Gaunt nodded vigorously in response, 'Yeah, I won't let you down.'

'Still, maybe it won't be necessary to fight at all,' added Tate thoughtfully.

'White men do not give up their gold easily,' remarked Aldo.

'Whites are scared to fight Apaches, at least if they've any sense. Once they see your men the townsfolk might be happy to hand over the money in return for being left in peace.'

Aldo considered this for a moment. 'Very well. When we get there, you can ask them. White men will not believe the word of an Apache, but they might believe another like themselves, one who steals and murders as they do.'

Tate let the insult pass and soon Maxwell came in to view. Aldo drew his men to a halt on an escarpment a short distance away. Tate peered through his spyglass and scanned the horizon.

'It looks like Callaghan's made a smart move,' he remarked.

'What can you see?' demanded Gaunt impatiently.

'They're building a barrier around the edge of the town. It's like a wall made up of waggons, tables, chairs, saddle-bags and stuff.' He passed the spyglass to Aldo and the Apache looked at the defences.

'If they defy us we will surround them, find where this wall is weak and then attack.'

Tate drew a white handkerchief from his pocket and Aldo handed him a spear. The outlaw bound the items together and galloped towards the town wielding his makeshift flag. He drew his mount to a halt just outside firing range and called out.

'Come and face me, Callaghan! I won't shoot, I just want to talk!'

Carver stood at the sheriff's elbow, the two men having just helped to complete the last section of the barrier. 'How come he's still alive?' demanded the station agent incredulously.

Luke shrugged in response. 'I guess he must have got the drop on Salinas and cut a deal with Aldo's men.'

'Well, you can't go out there. It must be some kind of trap.'

'Maybe, maybe not. The Apaches are brave, but they don't like to take chances and neither does Tate. Perhaps there's some way we can avoid a fight, or at least stall them for a while.' Callaghan then climbed carefully over the barrier and dropped down on to the other side. He walked slowly towards his adversary but then stopped while still some distance away.

'This is as far as I'll come. Say your piece, Tate.'

'I've come to make you an offer. Hand over the money and we'll leave. There's no need for anyone to get hurt. After all, you've got women and children behind there.'

'Killing the innocent hasn't bothered

you so far,' replied Callaghan.

'I just don't see the need to waste time on this thing.' Tate then gestured toward the barrier behind them. 'It looks very impressive, but it'll take more than a few tables and chairs to keep the Apaches out. Come on, you haven't got a chance.'

'The army will be here soon so we just have to hold out until then.'

'It'll take a couple of days by my reckoning. You won't hold Aldo's men off that long.' Tate leaned forward in his saddle. 'Come on, don't you know when to quit? Hand over the cash and this will all be over.'

'I can't decide by myself. We'll have to take a vote on it.'

Tate seemed amused by this. 'OK, go ahead. I'll give you fifteen minutes to let the people have their say, and then I want your answer.'

Callaghan climbed back over the barrier, eager hands reaching out to help him down. People crowded around him asking all kinds of questions and he raised his hands to quieten them. When there was silence he briefly explained Tate's proposal and his response. 'We don't have time to discuss this so I suggest we just take a vote. If a majority want to stand and fight, anyone who's not happy can then take their chances and ride out before the attack starts.'

To save time, voting was by a show of hands. When Callaghan asked how many were in favour of the deal offered by Tate there was no response. 'Don't be afraid. There's no shame in wanting to protect yourselves and your families,' he urged them.

A murmur ran through the crowd but still no one voted in favour.

'OK, how many against?'

A forest of hands went up with only a few abstentions. Callaghan swallowed hard.

'I just want to say now how proud I am to be your sheriff. Today you stood up to thieves and murderers. You stood up for the poor people who died on that stage, for justice and for the law. You should be proud, too.'

Suddenly, Christina was beside him, and she slipped her hand through his arm, kissing him on the cheek.

'What did I do to deserve that?'

'You made me feel proud also, proud to be on your side.'

'I just wish I could promise you're going to come out of this alive. If things were different, I'd like to promise you a lot more . . .'

She placed a finger against his lips. 'I know, but right now we face danger, and the time for promises will come when it is past. I have faith in you, Luke, as these people do and I believe we can win.'

The crowd began to disperse as they stepped down. Matt Carver then climbed to the top of the church tower so he could give Tate the people's answer. He did so with a single shot that landed near enough for the outlaw's horse to rear in response. Cursing as he struggled to regain control of his mount, Tate turned and galloped back to give Aldo and his followers the bad news.

4

'Those idiots down there want to fight!' declared Tate as he reached his companions.

'The white man's greed overcomes his wisdom,' replied Aldo.

The outlaw shook his head. 'That's not it. They've got some damn fool notion about doing the right thing with that money, which means not giving it to us. I can't understand it! The loot was insured anyway, so why bother?'

'Well, I can't say I'm sorry, not one little bit,' giggled Gaunt as he examined the long blade of his knife.

Aldo held out his hand for Tate's spyglass so he could study the town and its surroundings once more. Then he dismounted, crouched down and began to draw in the dirt with his spear. 'We will attack in a circle and surround them as the sky surrounds the earth,' he explained, scratching marks at various points on the ground. The chief then spoke to his men, giving instructions about where they should probe and try to break through the enemy's defences. The Apaches spread out as they began their advance, some armed with rifles while others carried bows, spears and clubs.

'I know you people prefer close combat with knives,' remarked Tate. 'You'll have to hit them hard with your firepower first.'

'You have nothing to teach us about how to fight,' replied Aldo contemptuously.

'I just don't want you to think these guys are going to be a pushover. They won't give up easily.'

'No, there are some white men with honour. Perhaps this Callaghan is one.'

Their pace quickened to a gallop as the Apaches let out their war cries. When they came within range and were met with volleys of rifle shots, some warriors shifted sideways in their

95

saddles to dodge the bullets. They returned fire, aiming to both hit their adversaries and dislodge parts of the barrier, splintering wood and splitting sandbags. Bowmen fired arrows over the top at points where the shots had come from. Groups of riders then split off as they strung out in a wide circle, almost encompassing the town. The Apaches were coming under heavy fire now and Tate saw several of them tumble from their horses. He breathed in the thickening smoke and stench of cordite as he fired his revolver at a bearded face below a battered Stetson that appeared above the barrier. The outlaw gave a grunt of satisfaction as the man fell back, his rifle falling from his hands.

At that moment, Aldo shouted an order as he rode among his men and the Apaches fell back. Tate was left exposed to a hail of bullets and jerked the reins of his horse abruptly as he hurried to join them. He cursed his allies for retreating so soon and remonstrated with Aldo as they reached the safety of the escarpment.

'What the hell are you doing? We were getting somewhere just then, I even got one of 'em myself!'

'Too many warriors were being lost. We are brave, but we do not throw our lives away.'

'We're fighting a battle here, damn it! People are going to get killed, and if you want a quick win you have to take chances.'

'Greed makes you careless, white man. The true warrior knows how to be patient, to hunt his enemy before he strikes.'

'Aren't you forgetting something? Time's not on our side, Aldo. There are troops heading this way and we can't be sure how soon they'll get here. It could be a couple of days but they might be quicker than that.'

'Enough! I command many warriors and each one is worth ten of you. I will not waste their lives because you fear the soldiers!'

'I never said I was afraid. I'm risking my neck out there the same as your men,' grumbled Tate defensively.

'We have learned where they are weak. That is where we will strike at the next attack. Then you will see how we overcome our enemies.'

'When will that be?'

Aldo glowered at him. 'When I say it will be. No more questions or I will cut out your tongue!' The chief then turned away and Tate knew better than to utter another word.

In Maxwell, a cheer had gone up at the sight of the Apaches retreating. Mick Harper started to climb up over the barrier to chase after them with his rifle but Callaghan pulled him back down.

'For God's sake, be careful. You can't fight them all!'

'Yeah but I got two of 'em, didn't I, Sheriff?'

'Sure you did, Mick. Your uncle would have been proud of you, but he'd also want you to live to fight another day and to keep his store going.'

The boy shrugged. 'I guess so. I was real scared at first, but then I got excited.'

Callaghan smiled at him. He wasn't such a bad kid after all. 'Yeah, well do me a favour and try to stay just a little scared, That way we might keep you alive. Now, we need more bullets. Go get some, will you?'

'What are our losses?' asked Carver as Mick Harper hurried away.

'Only two men dead but several others have arrow wounds. They can carry on fighting though.'

'It sounds like we've got the upper hand,' said the station agent, stroking the barrel of his Winchester.

Callaghan shook his head. 'Don't be fooled. Aldo's just probing for weak points in our defences. Apaches are brave but they value their lives and won't risk theirs any more than they have to.'

'Yeah, my old drill sergeant used to say that you don't win battles by dying for your country. You make the enemy die for his!'

'Well, they're just fighting for gain, and if we make it hard enough for them they might just give up and go away.' He clapped his friend on the shoulder. 'Come on, let's go check the barrier and make sure any gaps get filled in.'

There were several areas where sandbags had been pierced with arrows and items of furniture splintered. Callaghan kicked the remains of some chairs and asked 'How are we supposed to keep them out with this?'

The Reverend Samuel Endicott rose from the dust where he had been kneeling to comfort the widow of one of the men who been killed. 'We could take the pews from the church. They're much sturdier that most of the things we've been using, apart from the waggons of course.'

'That's a great idea, Reverend. We'd best hurry and round up some men. It won't be too long before Aldo tries again.'

The church was almost emptied of furniture within minutes and the pews were quickly stacked up against the weakest areas of the town's defences. When Callaghan and Carver took up their places again, Mick Harper was stumbling towards them carrying two boxes of ammunition. He dropped one as he came to a halt and the lid opened as it landed, revealing the contents.

The boy stared in embarrassment at the firecrackers with their long fuses, wrapped in brightly coloured paper.

'What are we supposed to do with these, Mick? Frighten the Apaches away with our big bangs?' asked an amused Carver.

'They'd certainly frighten their horses,' mused Callaghan. 'Besides, these things are dangerous and can easily blind or injure a man. Don't worry Mick. You did good bringing us our little surprise!'

'You could be right Luke,' said Carver as he picked up one of the firecrackers and stared at it. 'If we don't do something, I wouldn't count on us being around to use them on the fourth of July anyhow.'

* ★ ★

Aldo was now preparing his men for their next attack. He drew on the ground once more as he gave them their instructions. Tate watched intently and asked Billy what the chief was saying.

'He reckons there are some places where we might be able to get inside. It'd make things a whole lot easier.' The younger man made a stabbing gesture with his knife. 'I'd sure like to cut that sheriff's innards out with this thing and burn 'em in front of 'im. I'd save the heart 'til last, o' course. That'd be the best part.'

'I don't usually have much taste for your handiwork, Billy, but I'd be happy to make an exception for Callaghan.'

Their conversation was interrupted by the order to advance and the sound of an Apache war cry. Tate moved forward with the others, feeling more determined than ever. Callaghan had outsmarted him too many times, and now he was looking forward to his revenge.

The lookout posted in the church tower rang the bell and the townspeople took up their positions once more. The Apaches approached rapidly in a cloud of dust before spreading out. Stripped of their coloured wrappings, the fire-crackers lay hidden beneath scattered shrubs and thin coverings of dirt but linked together by a winding fuse looped through a tiny gap in the barrier.

The enemy came within range and the order was given to start firing, but they seemed harder to hit this time. Aldo focused his attack on areas where he knew the inhabitants' firepower was weak and some approached danger-ously close to the barrier. Painted warriors leaped from their horses to scramble over the top. One hurled a spear as he did so and it struck a man standing near Callaghan in the chest. He fell back with a choked cry as the sheriff swung around and fired his pistol. The Apache was hit in the face and crumpled over the barrier before his corpse was shoved roughly aside by Carver. Callaghan ordered the men in backup positions to move forward, reinforcing the defences. He lit the fuse as he did so and watched the small flame sizzle its way through the dirt. The pews from the church did their job, making it difficult for the Apaches to break through. Those who did were quickly shot down by the townspeople.

Then the firecrackers went off with a series of bangs and flashes. Horses bucked and reared in terror as their owners fought to control them before being picked off by rifle shots. Callaghan watched with grim satisfaction as one Apache was thrown to the ground, then struck by an exploding firecracker as he stumbled to his feet. He let out a shriek of agony as he fell once more with a scorching wound that burnt the skin off his chest.

Amid the clouds of smoke and confusion, four horsemen managed to clear the barrier, however. Callaghan recognised Aldo and Billy Gaunt among them. The younger man came charging towards him, firing a pistol but with a long-bladed knife clenched in his teeth. As the sheriff raised his gun to fire, a shot rang out from behind and the boy slumped forward as a bullet struck him between the shoulders. The knife fell from his mouth as he let out a cry and swayed in the saddle. In that moment, Callaghan saw the young boy he might have been, had fate not intervened, rather than the ruthless killer he had become. It gave Gaunt enough time to turn and flee, his horse clearing the barrier before the sheriff had a chance to finish him off.

It was then that he saw who had fired the bullet. Christina stood in the mêlée, frozen with shock. This was the first time she had ever shot, and possibly killed, anyone at close quarters. She slowly lowered the pistol clenched in both her hands as Aldo loomed up from behind and swept her on to his saddle. Callaghan let out a cry of rage as he began firing at the chief, but he hit another Apache warrior who passed in front of him at that moment. The fourth mounted warrior to clear the barrier was behind the sheriff and struck out with his club. Callaghan felt a searing pain in his skull before numbness enveloped his body and the sounds of battle faded to a distant murmur as he crumpled to the ground.

Tate had watched with mounting frustration as the townspeople fought back hard and the exploding firecrackers caused the attack to stall. Then Billy came towards him out of the smoke, his face deathly pale as he leaned over his horse's neck. The Apaches began to withdraw and the outlaw saw that the situation was hopeless.

'Come on, let's get you out of here,' he said roughly as he seized the bridle of his companion's horse and led him away.

'You wouldn't be goin' soft on me now, would yuh Tate? It's every man for himself. Ain't that what you taught me?'

'If you'd listened to me that well, you wouldn't have got shot,' replied the older man as the sounds of gunfire retreated behind them.

At last the two men reached safety and Tate gently lifted his companion down from his horse. The boy lay on the ground, deathly pale as the outlaw covered him with a blanket.

'It's bad, isn't it?'

Tate nodded. He was not a man who knew how to soften things, but he raised a canteen to his companion's lips and bade him drink.

'Thanks Tate. I'm glad I didn't have to kill you. Could you do me one last favour?'

'Sure, I reckon you've earned it.'

'Don't let them bury me like a white man . . . I want all my stuff in the grave and stones over it . . . Promise!'

'I promise, Billy.'

A brief smile of relief crossed Gaunt's lips before being replaced by a grimace of pain. His body stiffened and he let out his last breath in a long sigh. Tate swallowed hard and felt an unfamiliar stinging sensation behind his eyes. He put a hand up to his cheek and was surprised to find tears. The outlaw rarely felt much sentiment about anyone else, but he had been fond of Billy. The boy had looked up to him as a kind of mentor while at the same time being just as selfish and amoral as himself but with no pretence at being otherwise. The fact that he had been prepared to kill his boss to save his own skin, although with some regret, was a kind of compliment in a way. He was simply following the rules the older man had taught him.

Tate pulled the blanket over the dead boy's face, wondering if he would ever meet such a kindred spirit again. At that moment, a shadow passed over him and he looked up.

'He fought bravely as you promised', acknowledged Aldo.

'Yeah. It would have meant a lot to him to hear you say that. The kid asked for his body to be buried like an Apache's.'

'White men have a cross over them and prayers from your holy book.'

'Billy was raised by Apaches and today he fought like one and died like one. Isn't that enough?'

Aldo was silent for a moment and Tate met his gaze. After what seemed an eternity, the Mescalero leader nodded his consent and began to walk away. Turning his attention to other matters, Tate followed him.

'Taking the girl was a smart move. I think Callaghan's sweet on her and he'll negotiate to get her back.'

Aldo's eyes flashed with anger. 'She is to be my woman and no one else's!'

'I wasn't suggesting you actually give her back', Tate replied hastily. 'She can still be useful in getting what we want though, can't she?'

The Apache nodded thoughtfully. 'Yes, you will talk to Callaghan tomorrow. After tonight, the white man's pride will be broken and he will listen.'

'Why, what's gonna happen?' asked the puzzled outlaw.

Aldo smiled enigmatically. 'You will see.'

* * *

Back in Maxwell, Seth Fuller drew back from the barred window of the cell he shared with Judd Silver.

'What's happening out there?' asked his companion.

'It looks like they've driven off them Indians again.'

'We'd know about it by now if they hadn't.'

'Yeah, it beats me how you can be so cool about it. The thought of them savages hollerin' down the street makes

110

my blood run cold.'

Fuller peered out of the window again and noticed that there was no one guarding the post office. The men had moved up to reinforce those at the wall. Glancing down, he spotted something that excited him even more.

'Hey, Judd. Come over here 'cos you gotta see this!'

Silver got up from his bunk, wondering what could have triggered such a change in his friend's mood. Fuller then jabbed a grimy finger downwards through a gap in the bars and the gunman spotted the bundle of fire-crackers lying in the street below their window.

'I know you got some matches, Judd. We could blow the doors off this cell with what's down there!'

'Sure we could, but how are we gonna get it?'

Fuller fished in his pocket and held up a long piece of string. 'I always carry it around with me. It comes in handy sometimes.'

Silver felt a sudden surge of hope as he watched his friend tie a loose knot at one end and carefully lower the string through the barred window. Fuller guided it with painstaking slowness until at last he looped the knot over one of the fuses and pulled it tight. Silver held his breath as the precious cargo began its ascent and he offered a silent promise to the God he thought just might exist.

'Let me get out of here and I'll never steal anything or kill an innocent man or woman ever again.'

There was a moment when both men thought the bundle was not going to fit between the bars, but it did so with some tugging and squeezing. Fuller then drenched the bunk beds with the water they used for washing and turned them over on to their sides. Silver fumbled for his matches and lit one of the fuses, wedging the bundle under the barred door of the cell. The prisoners then jumped behind their beds and curled up against the wall. The blast sounded deafening when it came, but they were confident it would not be heard through the walls at the other end of town. Their greatest fear was that the cell might catch fire, trapping them inside, but the sparks which flew around them could not ignite the soaked bedding and they emerged safely to see that the once sturdy lock on the cell door had been reduced to a lump of black and twisted metal.

'There, what did I tell you?' cackled Fuller in triumph.

'I never doubted it for a second. Come on, let's get out of here!'

As both men headed for the street, Silver spotted his gun and holster lying on the sheriffs desk. He quickly buckled it on as his companion opened the jailhouse door and peered outside. There was no sign of anyone as both men emerged into the waning sunlight of a late afternoon.

Fuller headed straight for the post office. 'I bet there's no one guarding that money,' he said as his hand

113

touched the doorknob.

'Are you crazy? We need to get our horses from the stables and leave before anyone notices.'

'It'll only take a minute,' insisted the older man. As he began to open the door, Fuller felt his companion's revolver dig in to his ribs.

'You leave that cash where it is, Seth. I'd hate to have to kill you.'

'God damn it, what the hell's wrong with you? We could be rich as well as free!'

The gunman shook his head. 'I'm through stealing.'

'Well I ain't!' his companion shot back defiantly.

'Once we're outside town you can split and do whatever you want. Until then, just do like I tell you. Now move!'

There was a great deal of muttering as Fuller reluctantly let go of the door knob and moved down the street toward the stables. When they entered, he looked around for the best horse but Silver prodded him once more with his gun.

'We'll just take the ones we came with.'

'There are a couple over there that are much faster,' grumbled his companion.

'If our horses are slow, we'd best be on our way.'

Still muttering at what he regarded as Silver's attack of lunacy, Fuller saddled his horse, then bent down and frowned as he examined its leg.

'What's wrong now?'

'The goddamn horse is lame. Come on, see for yourself.'

As Silver lowered his gun and peered downwards in the dimly lit stable, Fuller reached up and grabbed the horseshoe he had spotted hanging on a nail. He was about to bring it crashing down on the gunman's skull when Silver sensed the flash of movement behind him, spun around and fired.

The bullet ripped through Fuller's chest at close range and the outlaw staggered backwards. The horseshoe was gripped tightly in one hand as the other clutched the scarlet stain spreading across his shirtfront. The dying man's knees buckled under him and his body sagged. Silver caught him as he fell.

'Why did you have to do that, Seth? I didn't want to kill you,' he said as he gently lowered him to the ground.

'I didn't want to kill you neither,' murmured Fuller. The fading light in his eyes could not disguise his look of puzzlement. 'You didn't want the money ... Why, Judd? Tell me ... why?' Then blood frothed from his lips, his eyes rolled back in their sockets and he let out his last breath.

'I made a deal, Seth, but not the kind you'd understand,' whispered Silver as he gave the dead man a reply that would never be heard. Then he quickly found his horse, swung himself into the saddle and galloped out of town before anyone discovered his absence.

Back at the other end of town,

Callaghan opened his eyes as the world slowly swam back into focus. The concerned faces were blurred for a moment before he recognized Martha Endicott, the minister's wife, who was holding a damp cloth to his forehead, Matt and Rosie Carver and young Mick Harper. Their voices, faint at first, grew louder as he sat up and then winced in pain.

'Take it easy, Luke. You took a mighty big blow there,' Carver told him.

The sheriff's stomach lurched as the moment of recollection produced a terrible, sick feeling that no words of comfort could assuage.

'Christina!' he cried.

'They won't hurt her, Sheriff. She's too valuable as a hostage,' said Mick Harper. Then he looked uncertainly at his companions. 'That's right, isn't it Mister Carver?'

'Of course it is.' The station agent sounded confident and he thought that the boy probably was correct, but no one could be sure.

'We've got to get her back,' insisted Callaghan as he struggled to his feet, the two women supporting him as he did so.

Carver shook his head. 'You're not thinking straight. If we attack them in open country, we'll be picked off one by one.'

Callaghan hesitated, knowing his friend was right, but instinct urged him on. 'I have to do something!' He looked around at them all pleadingly. 'I can't just sit here and wait, can I?'

'I don't know anything about battle tactics but it seems to me that that is exactly what you must do,' Martha Endicott told him. 'Those Apaches and that dreadful man Tate want what they came for. Surely the young lady's best chance is for us to keep them here fighting until the cavalry arrive, isn't it?'

Rosie Carver patted the sheriff's arm. 'She's right, Luke. If you men all go out there and get yourselves killed, Tate and the others will just ride in here and take the money. The rest of us won't be able to stop them — and didn't you say that Aldo has designs on Christina?'

Callaghan nodded. 'That's a very delicate way of putting it, but yes, he does.'

At that moment Arthur Norris came hurrying towards them, still carrying the rifle he used to guard the safe inside the post office where the payroll money was hidden.

'Judd Silver's escaped and he's killed Fuller!'

'Damn, that's all we need!' said Callaghan. 'Come on, you'd best show me.'

Norris led the way, explaining as he did so that he heard the two men lurking outside the post office following an almighty bang. He could not make out what they were saying, but it sounded like an argument. Silver rode out shortly afterwards and Norris went to investigate.

'So they didn't enter or make any attempt to steal the money?'

'No, Sheriff. I just can't figure it out.'

'Maybe they saw you inside with your shotgun,' suggested Carver.

'They couldn't have. I was hiding behind the counter.'

When they reached the jail, Callaghan bent down and examined the burnt-out remains of the firecracker. 'Well, at least we know how they did it, but it beats me how they managed to get hold of one.'

Norris then led them to Fuller's body and Callaghan stared at the mass of congealed blood over the hole in the outlaw's chest.

'They must have been pretty close up. I guess it was a case of dishonour among thieves.' Carver looked away from the corpse, disgust etched on to his features.

'More a case of self-defence,' replied Callaghan as he prised the horseshoe from the dead man's fingers. 'A blow from one of these things could cave your skull in.'

'I wonder why they argued,' mused Norris.

'The way I figure it, Fuller wanted to steal the money and Silver didn't. Fuller got sore, tried to get the jump on his buddy and Silver fired to protect himself.'

Carver shook his head and folded his arms over his chest. 'You won't convince me he's one of the good guys.'

'I never said that he was. Maybe he just got tired of killing and stealing, wants to try a different way.'

'Instead of arguing about it, shouldn't we be going after him?' asked Norris.

'We can't spare the men, not with what's going on here. I'm afraid we'll have to leave Silver to the army to hunt down,' sighed the sheriff.

'I'll go by myself and be back before nightfall. We can't just let him get away!' declared the exasperated station agent.

Callaghan clapped him on the shoulder. 'You're a good man, Matt, and I'd hate to lose you. Silver may be trying to reform a little, but he won't think twice about shooting another man to defend himself, and he's faster than you.'

'I know, but if we just leave it he'll be in Mexico before long.'

'Well, never mind. Either he'll settle down some place and do no more harm, or he'll go back to his old ways. If he chooses the second option, there'll be a bullet with his name on it or a noose waiting in a town nobody ever heard of. Now, let's get this varmint buried and those defences built up, shall we?'

Carver reluctantly agreed and the three men got back to work. Samuel Endicott was summoned to say a few words over the hapless outlaw's grave. He recited the twenty-third psalm and reminded the three reluctant mourners that the deceased man had a soul no matter what he had done, and might even have repented his misdeeds in the last moments of life. Callaghan seriously doubted this, but said nothing as he put his hat back on and returned to his post. Night would soon be falling, and some instinct told him that this might just turn out to be the most dangerous time of all.

5

The events of the day had exhausted Callaghan and despite his worries about Christina, the sheriff fell in to a deep sleep once he had seen to the defences and posted lookouts. Hours later, he felt himself dragged back to wakefulness by Mick Harper who was shaking him vigorously.

'Come on Sheriff! You gotta wake up!'

'What the hell is it?' he murmured groggily as he sat up. The smell that reached his nostrils and the crackling sound of burning wood told him all he needed to know. Thrusting aside his blanket, Callaghan was on his feet in seconds and ran outside, the youth following. The elaborately constructed wall of furniture was now a blazing pyre, its saffron flames illuminating the blue-black sky above them. The

124

townspeople dashed to and fro, their buckets of water spilling as they did so. Matt Carver had organized them into a line of willing helpers, but it was hopeless. Soon there would be nothing left.

'What about the lookouts?' Callaghan's foot bumped against soft flesh as he uttered these words and he glanced down to find his question answered by the sight of a corpse. The dead man had been struck in the throat by an arrow, his clawed hands raised in a vain attempt to pull it out before he breathed his last.

'The others are all the same,' Mick told him. 'Do you think the Apaches will come back soon?' the boy asked fearfully as he looked up at the night sky.

'They'll probably return when it's light. What have we got left that'll hold them off?'

'Apart from our guns, just a few barrels and sticks of furniture.'

The sheriff thought for a moment.

'All right. Go to the line and get three men to help you. Get enough stuff together to build a small barrier further down the street and block it off. Do the same with the small alleys running off it.'

'Do you think we still have a chance, Sheriff?'

'Maybe. I'll post men on rooftops and at windows. The barriers will slow the Apaches down and we can pick them off more easily that way. If we're lucky the cavalry will be here by sundown.'

Callaghan felt a stab of guilt as Mick ran off to do his bidding. It was wrong to raise false hopes in the lad. They could certainly keep the enemy at bay for a while using these methods, but not for long. He slumped to his knees, his head in his hands. The inhabitants of Maxwell would be dead before noon and there was nothing he could do about it. The people voted to fight because they trusted him, and in his stubborn pride he had let them down.

Callaghan's only hope was that he could delay Aldo and Tate long enough to allow the army time to catch up with them. At least then there was a chance Christina might be freed.

'Don't blame yourself, Sheriff. No man could have done more to protect this town and its people.'

Callaghan looked up at Samuel Endicott. The minister was a sight to behold, his suit crumpled and face blackened with smoke, but he had not lost the air of dignity and inner peace he always carried with him.

'That's kind of you, Reverend, but the truth is we wouldn't be in this spot if I'd invoked my authority as sheriff and handed over the money.'

Endicott nodded. 'No one would have blamed you had you chosen to do that, but there is another truth to consider. This town would have slowly withered and died of shame, no man able to look another in the eye or speak of honour and courage without the words sticking in his throat.'

127

'What about the children? It'll be my fault if they're slaughtered or brought up as Apaches!'

The minister squeezed his arm reassuringly and gently but firmly raised him from his knees. 'They're all well hidden in cellars and under floorboards with instructions to keep quiet and enough food to last a couple of days. The Apaches will have better things to do than go hunting for them when the cavalry are hot on their heels.'

'Well, that's a relief, at least.'

'It is through them that this town's sacrifice will be remembered. After all, who would now remember the Alamo if the folks had all surrendered when the chance was first offered to them?'

Callaghan found himself laughing despite their predicament. 'I quite like the idea of being a William Travis or Davy Crockett.'

At that moment, Matt Carver approached them. 'It's no good, Luke. The fire's taken everything. Mick told me your plan but I didn't have the heart to tell him that it'll just buy us a little more time.'

The sheriff shrugged. 'Maybe there's no harm in letting him have hope for a while.'

Endicott held up his bible. 'And a little faith too, gentlemen. Let's not forget that.'

'Yeah, well I guess now wouldn't be a bad time to start praying,' said Carver.

'There's never a bad time to do that,' the minister replied before going off to comfort his congregation.

As dawn smouldered on the horizon, Callaghan made what preparations he could for the attack that was bound to come. He watched the sunrise with all his senses on edge and it was with some surprise that he saw a small party approach under a white flag, led by Aldo and Tate. The riders reached the edge of town, formed a line and then parted. Christina emerged from behind, her hands and feet bound to the reins and stirrups of a pale horse. Callaghan immediately stepped forward and she shook her head in warning as her eyes met his.

'That's far enough,' Tate warned him. 'Come any closer and I'll shoot her in the back.' He held a rifle in the crook of his arm and it was pointed straight at her.

'What do you want?' demanded the sheriff, reluctantly standing his ground.

Tate prodded Christina in the ribs with the gun's muzzle. 'Go on, you tell him.'

The girl drew a deep breath and then began. 'They want you to hand over the money. If you do that, they will leave peacefully. If not, you will all be killed.'

'What about you?'

Christina closed her eyes tightly and put her head down. She began to sob quietly and Callaghan noticed that her hair was dishevelled and her clothes torn.

'She is to be my woman,' said Aldo decisively.

'Let her go and you've got a deal.'

The Apache said nothing but shook his head.

'Come on, that's the good part. She hasn't told you everything that will happen if you refuse,' said Tate.

Callaghan felt sickness rise in his stomach but he had to know. 'Go on, tell me.'

Christina looked up once more and he saw where the tears had left tracks in her dirty face. She struggled to compose herself for a moment and then continued.

'I will be given to Aldo's men, each in turn. They guessed that you have hidden the children and Aldo says that he will leave a few men behind so that for every hour you delay him, a child will be found and killed.'

A murmur ran through the group of townspeople who had gathered around the sheriff and a woman, the mother of a young child, began to sob.

'For God's sake, Sheriff, give these heathens what they want!' a man called out.

'How long have we got to decide?'

Aldo then thrust the spear he was carrying into the ground. 'Enough talk! You decide now or I do all that has been said!'

Callaghan glanced around at the onlookers. 'You won't need to take a vote this time, Sheriff. Folks know when they're beaten,' said the man who had called out earlier.

Matt Carver was at his side and squeezed his shoulder gently. 'We've no choice, Luke. No man can stomach knowing that if he fights hard enough, children will die because of it.'

'All right, we'll do as you say,' conceded Callaghan. The words came out in a whisper, his voice suddenly weak.

Carver took some men and went off to the post office to collect the saddle-bags of cash, which were then dumped in front of the enemy. Aldo gave a smile of satisfaction as he signalled to the men he had brought with him to take one each. Then he drew his spear out of the ground, held it horizontally in both hands and snapped it. The sound of wood splintering was loud in the silence and the Apache leader tossed the pieces into the dirt at Callaghan's feet.

'You see, white man. You are not so strong but break easily, like my spear.'

The sheriff watched helplessly as Christina was led away. She turned once to look back at him and then slumped dejectedly over her horse's neck. Tate was the last to leave, favouring them with a mock salute before he rode off.

'I guess we could try tracking them,' suggested Callaghan with more conviction than he felt.

'They'd spot us a mile off,' replied Carver. 'We'll get her back, Luke. You just have to be patient until the army gets here.'

'They'll be half way to Mexico by then,' said the sheriff as he turned away in bitterness. Then a sudden thought struck him. 'No, maybe they won't,' he murmured to himself.

'What is it, Luke?' asked the station agent.

'Come with me, we need to look at that map on the wall in the post office.'

The two men set off down the street, Callaghan striding ahead as his friend hurried to catch up. Ignoring a dejected Arthur Norris, the sheriff lifted the map down from the wall and placed it on the counter where he began to study it carefully.

'What are you looking for?' asked Carver.

'That hideout we were taken to. Where is it?'

Carver traced his finger along a low-lying range of hills. 'It must be somewhere around here.'

'That's more or less what I figured. Now, they've got a good stash of weapons back there for sale. Aldo won't want to head for the border without them, whatever Tate thinks.'

'They'll have to go around in a big loop to do that,' said Carver.

'Exactly. Now, if we trace the most direct route to the border from the hideout we end up somewhere around here.' Callaghan jabbed his finger at the area around a small border town.

'That's San Elizario, right on the Rio Grande. It's a stage stop less than twenty miles from El Paso.'

'If we're underway by nightfall, we'll be there before Aldo and Tate, which gives us time to wait for the cavalry.'

The hours passed, people brought their children out of hiding, homes and businesses were repaired to the sounds of hammering and sawing as the town returned to some semblance of normality. Then, at mid-afternoon a cloud of dust appeared on the horizon and lines of mounted men in blue uniforms slowly became visible as a cavalry troop approached the town.

As the soldiers came to a halt, Callaghan studied their leader, a stocky, swarthy individual who wore a sergeant's stripes on the sleeve of his dusty tunic.

'Where's your officer?' the sheriff asked.

The man jerked his thumb backwards. 'We buried him out there in the desert. Lieutenant Colley was from back east someplace and fresh outta West Point. I guess some damn fool general figured the dry air of the desert would do 'im good on account of his delicate health, but a man who can't stand heat is liable to pick up fevers out here.' There was an awkward pause before he went on to introduce himself. 'I'm Sergeant Jefferson Pike and I'm in charge o' these here men.'

Pike then scratched his greying beard with a beefy hand and indicated the tall civilian who rode beside him.

'This is Mister Bert Gorman, a Wells Fargo detective . . . '

'Thank you, Sergeant,' Gorman cut in. 'So, what's been going on here, Sheriff?'

Callaghan felt the man's hard brown eyes appraising him coolly from beneath their hooded lids. Gorman's

136

tall, spare figure leaned forward in the saddle and he listened attentively as the lawman recounted the events of the past few days.

'It's unfortunate that you allowed the prisoners in your custody to escape, Sheriff, most unfortunate, not to mention the stolen money handed back to thieves.'

'It seems to me that without the efforts of Callaghan and these good folks here, we wouldn't have a hope in hell o' catchin' the varmints and gettin' the money back!' protested Pike.

'Quite so, Sergeant. I'm not trying to apportion blame, but it is a most unfortunate turn of events following Tate's initial capture, as I'm sure the sheriff will agree.'

'Yeah, it's damned unfortunate, especially for Christina Salinas. The point now is to get her rescued, the money returned and Tate under arrest.'

'I agree,' conceded Gorman before turning to address Pike. 'Now Sergeant, what do you say to an hour's rest for your men before we head for San Elizario, as the sheriff suggests?'

Pike nodded curtly and gave the order to dismount. The detective then turned his attention to Matt Carver who had come to stand beside Callaghan.

'And who might you be?'

'My name's Carver. I'm the station agent here.'

'I shall need to interview you about your role in this affair, Mister Carver,' said Gorman as he climbed down from his horse. 'I suggest you keep this man in custody until then, Sheriff.'

Callaghan finally exploded. 'Damn you, Gorman. Have you listened to a word I said? Matt almost got himself killed trying to bring Tate to justice!'

'I always listen very carefully to what people tell me, Sheriff. One of the most puzzling features of this whole business is how Tate and his men found out about the large amount of money being carried on that stage. The driver and the guard knew what they were carrying, but no one else. Carver must have known these men well, and they will have trusted him. Who was in a better position to find out?'

'You must be crazy!' protested Carver. 'Why would I risk my neck to get that money back if I was paid to help steal it in the first place?'

'What better way to cover your tracks once the plan went wrong?'

Callaghan forced himself to calm down. 'Now look, Mister Gorman. I know you have your job to do and need to consider all the possibilities when you investigate a crime, but this is just pure speculation. I've known Matt a long time and I can assure you that he's incorruptible. Everyone in this town will say the same thing.'

Gorman's thin lips drew in a smile. 'In my experience, Sheriff, no one is incorruptible. However, if your friend comes along with us to San Elizario so I can keep an eye on him, I am prepared to waive my request for custody.'

'Is that OK with you, Matt?'

'Sure Luke. I was going to come anyway.'

Gorman removed his derby hat and ran a hand through a head of jet black hair that came to a widow's peak above his high forehead. He smiled at both men as he led his horse over to the stables, and Matt scowled at his retreating back.

'I don't like that guy one bit. When I hear his silky voice with its accusations and look at him in his fancy suit, it makes me think he'll put anyone in jail just to make a big name for himself.'

'He certainly has a way of rubbing people up the wrong way, but then he is a detective. Maybe being suspicious of everybody comes with the job.'

'Along with seeing crimes where there aren't any. How does he know Tate and his gang didn't just get lucky? Maybe they had no idea what that stage was carrying. After all, I didn't.'

Callaghan clapped him on the shoulder. 'I know you didn't, Matt, but maybe somebody did tell them, or Tate

140

at least. There could be more to this, and Gorman, unpleasant though he is, could be just the man to sniff it out.'

'Well, he certainly seems determined to catch up with Tate and Aldo, that's something at least.'

★ ★ ★

Aldo and his men, meanwhile, were just leaving their hideout, having returned to collect the weapons. Tate had been keen to get across the border straightaway, but the thought of the additional money all those rifles would bring in held an allure that overcame his caution. The only problem now was how to get rid of his unwanted allies. The Mescalero leader rode just ahead with Christina beside him, and the outlaw could hear their conversation clearly.

'Soon I will be as rich as any Mexican or white man,' Aldo began. 'The rifles will bring much gold. You shall not live as a squaw.'

'That's easy to say now you don't have to carry out your threat and give me to your men.'

'Not so, I knew those words would frighten Callaghan who looks at you with hungry eyes. No, you belong only to Aldo.'

Christina flinched and drew away sharply as the Apache reached out to stroke her hair. 'You may force yourself upon me but I will never belong to you, never!'

Aldo drew back as she spat the words out at him. 'Many of my own tribe would willingly give themselves to me, but I have chosen you. You will accept this. You will accept it when I come to you tonight!' Then he rode on abruptly.

Tate drew alongside her in his place. 'We'll make camp in a few hours. What will you do then? Scratch his eyes out?'

'What do you care? You're as bad as he is.'

The outlaw shrugged in response. 'Maybe I am, but then again, maybe not. I don't like to see a woman with your spirit sacrificed to a man like him. There might be something I can do to help.'

Christina looked at him suspiciously through narrowed eyes. 'Why should you help me?'

Tate handed her a canteen and signalled for her to drink. She felt the knife taped to the back of it and glanced around to ensure she was not observed. She then quickly concealed it beneath her clothing.

'It belonged to Billy, but I figured you could use it,' the outlaw said quietly as she passed the canteen back to him.

'You still haven't answered my question.'

'Does it matter why I'm giving you a chance?'

Now it was her turn to shrug. 'I guess not, but I imagine it's because you want to get rid of Aldo, and it's easier to let someone else do it for you.'

'Just take my advice and let him get his pants down first,' whispered the outlaw before he rode ahead to catch up with Aldo, leaving her alone with her thoughts.

'Well, we got the money back. When do I get my share?'

Aldo did not look at his companion as he made his reply. 'You will get it when I choose to give it to you, and not before.' The Apache then asked, 'What were you saying to the woman?'

Tate shrugged. 'I was just advising her to make the best of things. After all, you're going to be rich when all this is over.'

Dusk fell and they made camp. Once they had eaten, Christina was shown to a sheltered spot away from the others and given some blankets. A fire was lit and the young warrior who was with her gestured for her to lie down. She had learned that he was called Chico, and that Aldo considered him one of his best men. He grinned unpleasantly at her as he moved away into the shadows. A victory had been won, and the men were celebrating with whiskey and mescal. Aldo was now their hero, and she knew he would remain drinking with them for a time. Eventually he would come to her and she lay with every muscle tensed, the knife gripped in her right hand beneath the blanket.

Eventually, she heard shuffling footsteps and a figure loomed over her in the firelight. Aldo tossed the half bottle of whiskey he had been clutching to the ground and wiped his mouth with the back of his hand. Christina drew the blanket aside and he saw that she had removed her outer clothing. Aldo sank to his knees beside her and she placed an arm around his neck. He smiled and brought his lips close to hers as his hands groped her body. She felt the knife in her free hand and buried the blade in his chest up to the hilt. Christina withdrew it and his eyes widened in surprise as he looked down at the gaping wound. She stabbed him several more times, her desperation to escape whipping her into a frenzy.

Aldo's reflexes were slowed by drink, and he was no match for a desperate and determined woman. Blood spurted from his wounds, leaving him too weak even to rise.

Christina stepped back from him as he crawled towards her, his hands reaching up to seize her throat. Then he slumped forward and lay still. She stood for a moment, as if rooted to the spot, but fear of discovery overcame her shock and she moved quickly to dress herself and find a swift horse which she then led away from the camp before mounting it and riding off into the night.

Aldo's men made the grisly discovery of their leader's body at dawn, and there was an animated discussion about what they should do next. Tate understood little of their language but gathered that they were planning to hunt down Christina and put her to death very slowly and painfully.

'My friends,' he addressed them. 'Yesterday your chief gave me his last command, to ride with you to San Elizario and get the best possible price for his rifles. That can't be done if everyone is busy chasing the girl.'

It was the young brave called Chico who answered as he spat contemptuously on the ground. 'You think only of gold, white man. We must avenge Aldo.'

'Of course you must, but she's just one woman. How many of you can it take to capture her? You can also honour Aldo by carrying out his command and selling those rifles.'

There were murmurs among the group as Chico translated these words for the benefit of those who had not understood. Sensing that they were now less certain, he pressed home his advantage.

'Look, I've seen you fight, and it would only take two reliable men to find this wretched woman and deal with her. The rest of us can then sell these rifles and carry out your chief's wishes.'

There was a further brief discussion

before it seemed that a consensus was reached. Then Chico turned back to Tate. 'We will do as you say, but be warned. Betray us, and you will suffer as the woman will suffer.'

Tate nodded slowly in response. There was no doubt in his mind that the threat would be carried out. He would have to continue to tread carefully, very carefully in deed.

Christina had ridden desperately throughout the night, aware that her only hope was to put as much distance between herself and Aldo's men as possible, for she had no doubt that they would seek revenge for his death. The pinto she had stolen sweated and snorted beneath her. The poor creature was getting weary, and she decided her best option would be to let him rest and walk for a few miles. But before she could slow down, she reached a slope and her tired mount lost his balance as the sands shifted beneath them. He bucked and reared as he fell and she was thrown up into the air — she had just a blinding glimpse of sunlight before the ground rose to meet her and darkness descended.

When she awoke, it was to the sound of shallow breathing and a faint whinnying sound from the pinto. The horse's eyes were widened in pain, and it was clear that one of his legs was broken. There was nothing for it but to put the poor creature out of its misery. Christina had no pistol but took the knife she carried and slit a vein in the pinto's neck. She then knelt beside him, whispering softly and stroking the animal as he died. Standing up, she set off resolutely to walk, hoping against hope that she had travelled far enough already to be out of reach.

The two men who followed on fresh horses that had rested overnight soon picked up her trail and narrowed the distance between them. They came across the dead pinto when Christina had been walking for almost three hours. She stumbled determinedly onwards under the blazing sun, heading

149

towards a canyon where she hoped she might be able to find a safe hiding place as well as some cool shade. She reached the foot of it and began to climb upwards, ignoring the ache she felt in every limb. Her water was almost gone, but even dying of thirst out here was preferable to what Aldo's men would do to her. She heard horses in the distance and looked around, shading her eyes from the harsh sunlight with a grimy hand. She could barely make out the two figures who were rapidly approaching, but they appeared to be carrying spears and one of them pointed in her direction. Summoning all her strength, she desperately tried to scramble up the slope. She seemed to be making some progress when she somehow slipped and, unable to find a foothold, slid back down to the bottom.

The two Apaches were only a short distance away now and Christina could see their painted faces. There was only one thing left to do. Reaching for her knife, she raised it high in both hands and prepared to plunge it into her heart. At that moment, a shot rang out and one of the Apaches tumbled from his horse. His companion let out a cry of alarm and raised his spear before another shot followed and he too fell to the ground.

Christina's benefactor strode down the slope and gently extended a hand to help her to her feet. She let out a small cry, unsure of whether to be relieved or not.

'It's OK, you won't come to any harm from me,' said Judd Silver.

She drank greedily from the canteen he handed her. 'What are you doing out here?'

'I was just about to ask you the same thing.'

Christina briefly explained how the town had surrendered and handed over the stolen payroll before describing how she had managed to kill Aldo and escape. Silver nodded slowly as he listened to her account.

'So, what are you going to do with

me?' she asked suspiciously.

'I told you, you've nothing to fear from me.'

'Then you'll let me go before re-joining Tate?' she asked hopefully.

'I'm not interested in Tate or his damned money.'

Christina shook her head. 'I don't understand.'

'I'm not sure I do either. Anyway, it was lucky for you my horse went lame and had to rest up. Otherwise I'd have crossed the border before now. As it is, we'll take those horses and I'll escort you across.'

'I'm not sure I can trust a man like you.'

Silver shrugged in response. 'I can understand that, but what choice do you have?'

Christina let out a sigh of resignation. 'None, I guess.'

6

Callaghan and his companions rode wearily through the desert towards San Elizario. Pike's men had ridden hard to reach Maxwell in the first place, and this second journey was taking its toll on both the riders and their horses. The burly sergeant removed his hat and mopped the sweat from his balding pate with a large handkerchief.

'I'm none too sure about this plan of yours, Sheriff. It seems to me them darned Apaches could catch us up in open country if we keep goin' at this pace.'

'Can't we go any faster?' demanded Gorman.

'Sure, if you want the horses to die underneath us we can,' replied Pike with obvious sarcasm.

'Do you have any ideas?' asked Callaghan.

The sergeant unfolded a crumpled map from a pocket in his tunic and pointed to it. 'There's a low-lyin' range about five miles up ahead. A narrow track runs through it and them Apaches will pass that way. It seems to me our best chance is to hide out there and attack when they arrive.'

'It seems I was a little hasty, Sergeant. It sounds like your plan has a good chance of success,' conceded Gorman.

'Well, it won't be as easy as shootin' fish in a barrel, our enemy bein' pretty smart, but I reckon we'll win.'

'I hope your men will bear in mind that Aldo has a hostage,' commented Callaghan.

'Until recently, the girl was riding with a group of bandits led by her brother, was she not?' asked Gorman.

'Against her will,' Callaghan reminded the detective. 'She also risked her own neck to save innocent people. The least we can do is try to avoid shooting her.'

'We can't afford to be sentimental,'

insisted Gorman. 'Tate must be apprehended at all costs, so I suggest you stop mooning over the Salinas girl and remember where your duty lies!'

The detective had been riding on Callaghan's left and Pike on his right. The sheriff swung around in one smooth motion, his fist smashing into Gorman's jaw. The blow sent the other man tumbling from his horse and he lay sprawling in the hot sand.

The detective slowly staggered to his feet and his dazed expression soon switched to one of anger. He reached for his gun only to find that Callaghan's was already out of its holster and pointing at him.

'I've just about had enough of you and your smart mouth, Gorman. If you ever decide to go for that holster again, I'll be happy to fire at you.'

Gorman made a show of dusting himself off and wiped away the trickle of blood that ran from the corner of his mouth. 'You struck an officer of the law, Callaghan. What did you expect me to do?' His tone was defiant yet tinged with fear.

'I'm an officer of the law too,' Callaghan reminded him. 'Show me a little respect and I'll extend you the same courtesy.'

'Tate will be your prisoner,' Pike added as the detective climbed back on to his horse, 'but until we fight off the Apaches and he's recaptured, this here is a military operation and that puts me in charge. I'd be obliged if you'd remember that.'

Gorman said nothing but nodded curtly and rode on ahead. Pike then turned to Callaghan. 'That goes for you, too, Sheriff. If there's any blows to be struck, I'll give 'em out myself — though I reckon he had it comin', and I must admit, it cheered me no end to see you put him on his ass. Just try not to do it again.'

The range proved to be a little further ahead than anticipated, and they were glad to reach its slopes, move to higher ground and find some shade beneath the overhanging rocks. Pike proved to be adept at finding sheltered spots with a good view of the path below, and there were a couple of large caves in which the horses could be tethered out of sight.

They settled down to wait, unsure of when the Apaches would arrive. It could be that evening, but was more likely to be the following day. Towards sunset, however, the lookout reported the approach of two riders. Pike peered through his spyglass and identified that it was a man and a woman. Then he passed it to Callaghan.

'I recognize the man, it's Judd Silver and the woman . . . it's Christina! She must have escaped, thank God.'

'At the risk of causin' some offence, Sheriff, can I ask what she'd be doin' with that killer if she's as innocent as you say?' asked the sergeant.

Callaghan shrugged. 'He must have found her in the desert after she got away. We'll find out soon enough.'

Pike waited until the pair were

passing below his men, and then called out. 'Stop right where you are, you're surrounded! Judd Silver, undo that gun belt real slow and let it drop to the floor. Then raise your hands. Miss Salinas, you put your hands up too, please.'

Silver hesitated for a moment until, at a signal from Pike, his men rose and pointed their rifles at him. Cursing softly under his breath, he slowly did as he was ordered while Christina raised her hands.

Pike sent four of his men down, two to escort the pair up to the top and two to take their horses. One of them picked up Silver's weapon and bound his hands. Christina was also searched and her knife taken. The cavalryman looked at her suspiciously. 'Your knife has blood on it,' he remarked.

'It's from the Apache chief who led the attack on Maxwell. What was I supposed to do, let him rape me?'

The soldier reddened with embarrassment. 'I'm sorry . . . Sheriff

Callaghan did say you'd been captured.'

At that moment, Callaghan came running down toward her. 'Christina, you're safe!' They embraced and remained holding on to each other tightly until one of the soldiers pointed out that they were in an exposed position and needed to move quickly. Silver was shoved in front of them at gunpoint, his hands still raised.

'Did he hurt you at all?' asked Callaghan.

Christina shook her head. 'No, two of Aldo's men came after me and he shot them. I wouldn't be here otherwise.'

'Then I guess I'm obliged to him, but he's still dangerous to be around.'

'What will happen to him now?' she asked as the sheriff took her hand and led her up to safety.

'He'll hang, I guess.'

'It seems a shame somehow,' she remarked wistfully.

'I wouldn't waste any tears. He's not as bad as Tate, but he's killed innocent people and he's going to have to pay for it.'

When they reached the top, Christina greeted Matt Carver warmly, glad to find that he, too, was still alive. Then Callaghan introduced her to Pike and Gorman. 'Our detective here may have some questions for you, but he's a suspicious man by nature and likely to be a little insensitive. Let me know if he gives you any trouble.'

Gorman raised his hands in a placatory gesture. 'My questions can wait, Miss Salinas. I gather you've had quite an ordeal, so why don't you go rest a while?'

She nodded her thanks and one of the soldiers led her away to one of the caves where food and water were being stored. The detective then pointed in Silver's direction. 'With your permission, Sergeant, I wouldn't mind questioning that man right away. He will no doubt have valuable information about the robbery.'

Pike scratched his beard. 'Go ahead.

Let me know if you find out anything useful.'

Gorman quickly made his way to the cave where Silver was now being guarded. It was one he shared with the horses, and the detective wrinkled his nose at the smell. After introducing himself, he sat himself down on a rock in front of the prisoner.

'Well, well. It seems you've had quite a reversal of fortune, Silver. I rather thought you'd be in Mexico by now.'

'Have you come to gloat, Mister Gorman?'

'On the contrary, I might be able to do you some good.'

Silver leaned forward, suddenly interested. 'How's that?'

'Well, let me see. There seem to be some mitigating circumstances in your case. You didn't attempt to steal the money back when you escaped, and it appears you prevented Fuller from doing so. I take it you didn't harm the girl either.'

'I killed a couple of Apaches who

were after her. I was helping her get to safety when I was caught.'

Gorman removed a silver flask from inside his jacket and took a swig. 'I hope you like brandy.'

Silver took the proffered flask and helped himself to a generous gulp before handing it back.

'Does all this mean I can get some sort of pardon?'

'Not exactly, but it does give you some credibility if you decide to turn state's evidence. You see, there's one important part of the puzzle missing.'

Silver was nonplussed. 'What puzzle?'

'The puzzle of how Tate knew that the Wells Fargo stage you robbed was carrying an army payroll. Very few people did know, and they were all sworn to secrecy, including the driver and the guard.'

Silver thought hard for a moment. 'Tate plays his cards pretty close to his chest. I'm just trying to recall what he said about it before we did the job.'

'Well, let me see if I can jog your

memory. What do you know about the station agent, Matt Carver?'

Silver shrugged. 'Not much. He's a big pal of Callaghan's and helped him track us down after the robbery.'

'It seems to me he was in a unique position to obtain information. He knows all the drivers and the guards. They eat and drink at his place, so someone must have let something slip. I'm sure of it, but I just need confirmation.'

Silver shook his head dejectedly. 'I'd be lying if I said Tate ever mentioned his name. I can't send an innocent man to jail just to save my own neck.'

'Well, no one's asking you to lie,' conceded Gorman reluctantly. 'I need an answer, Silver, and that answer could mean the difference between you going to jail for a few years or swinging from a rope, so I suggest you think hard.'

Silver suddenly brightened. 'Maybe it was the guard or the driver. If you give me their names, maybe . . . '

'They're both dead, and evidence

against dead men isn't worth anything,' said Gorman curtly. 'Maybe Tate did buy information and kill the seller to cover his tracks, but for your evidence to be worthwhile it has to be against someone who's alive to take the consequences and who'd otherwise get away with it.'

The detective then stood up. 'For what it's worth, I still think Carver could be the man I'm looking for. Think about it, Silver, and let me know if you suddenly remember something.'

The gunman watched the detective walk back out of the cave and into the fading light of dusk. A lie might save him from the gallows, but framing an innocent man was a coward's way out, and whatever his faults, Judd Silver was no coward. No, he would have to look out for some chance to escape.

'I hear you did some good. Christina says you saved her life.' Matt Carver was standing over him, holding out a metal cup. 'I figured you could use some coffee.'

'Thanks, that tastes good.'

'What happened with Fuller?'

The gunman shrugged. 'He came at me from behind so I had to shoot him.'

'What did he do that for?'

Silver seemed almost embarrassed by his reply, 'He wanted to take the payroll money and I stopped him.'

Carver shook his head in puzzlement. 'That's what Luke figured, but I can't make you out. You killed and robbed those poor folks on the stage, so why didn't you take the money when you had the chance?'

Silver looked up at him and grinned. 'You want it all black and white, don't you? Life's not always like that, and people aren't either.'

'I guess not. What did Gorman want, anyway?'

'He seems to think you had something to do with the robbery, that you were the one who told Tate about the payroll.'

'I never knew a damn thing about that payroll!' insisted the station agent.

'Gorman accused me of being involved the minute he arrived in Maxwell.'

Silver raised his eyebrows. 'Really? Well, he offered me a deal. If I turn you in, I can avoid the rope.'

Carver paled visibly. 'What did you tell him?'

'The truth: that I have no idea where Tate got his information from, but I got the impression Gorman's not too bothered about what's true and what isn't. He just wants a loose end tied up.'

Carver shifted his feet uncertainly. 'It must have been a tempting offer.'

The gunman met his gaze. 'It was, but you can relax. I'm not gonna sell you out.'

The station agent nodded. 'I appreciate it. Let me know if you need anything.'

The evening passed and night fell. Pike posted lookouts, but as the hours crept by until dawn, there was no sign of any movement below. Callaghan slept only fitfully, half expecting the Apaches to come creeping silently up

166

the path towards them, slit the throats of the sentries and slaughter the rest before they had time to react. He awoke with a start as the sun's first rays began warming the earth. Throwing his blanket aside, he stretched his limbs which were stiff after a night on the hard ground. Christina lay nearby, still sleeping although the sounds she made suggested that her dreams were no more peaceful than his had been.

Meanwhile, Chico and his men were setting off after having made camp for the night. He was concerned that the two men he had sent after Christina had not yet returned.

'She's no match for an Apache, but she's a resourceful girl who knows the desert,' Tate told him. 'Maybe it's taken them longer than they expected to track her down.'

Chico nodded slowly. 'It may be as you say, but we'll follow their trail and soon we shall know.'

It was not long before they came across buzzards feeding on the remains of the horse Christina had stolen. The bones had been almost picked clean. Chico's features darkened with rage when he came across the bodies of the two men he had sent after her. He leaped down from his horse and chased away the buzzards that were feeding on their corpses.

'This is what comes of listening to the white man!' He pointed an accusatory finger at Tate.

'Aw, c'mon Chico! You can see those men have been shot. She must have had some luck, come across someone who helped her. How could anyone have predicted that?'

The Apache was silent for a moment. 'This is true, but they cannot be far away and soon we shall find them.' Chico ordered that the men be buried quickly, then mounted his horse and galloped on ahead of them.

The trail led them to the low-lying range but Chico drew his men to a halt as his horse stood, its nose twitching.

Tate came alongside him. 'What is it?

Why have we stopped?'

The Apache pointed to the ground ahead of them, dismounted and crept forward to examine the tracks more closely. Then he rose from his haunches and strode back to his mount before giving the signal to turn around.

'What are you doing? The way to San Elizario is straight through there!'

'It is a trap! The tracks stop, then there are more going up,' and he pointed to the top of the range.

Tate looked up, shielding his eyes from the sun's rays. 'I don't see a damned thing!' he protested.

Chico held out his hand for the gunman's spyglass and peered through it, scanning the top of the range. Then he paused, handed the instrument to Tate and urged him to look.

'I just saw a couple of flashes.'

'Yes, it is the sun on the rifles of white men. The soldiers have not followed us, but knew where to come. This Callaghan, he thinks like an Apache.'

'Maybe we could just run through real fast,' suggested Tate.

'That would be foolish. Many will die. No, we go around in a circle.'

'They'll still be ahead of us,' warned the gunman.

'Yes but on open land. Then we will close the circle and crush them!' Chico then bunched his hand in to a fist to illustrate his point.

'But that'll take days! What if there's not enough food and water?' protested Tate.

'There will be enough. The Apache are strong.' Chico fixed him with a hard stare. 'If you are weak you will be left behind.'

High above them, Pike waited impatiently. He had seen the Apaches about to enter the path below, stop and then retreat.

'Goddamn it, they've spotted us!'

'What do you think they'll do now?' asked Carver anxiously.

'They won't come through here, that's for sure. It'd be suicide. They'll either turn back to their hideout or go the long way around. Either way, we'll face a hard battle at the end of it.' The burly sergeant thought for a moment and then shouted out to those below.

'Hey, any Apaches down there speak English?'

Chico rode forward. 'Speak, I am listening!'

'Look, all we want is for you to hand over Tate and the money he stole. If you're gonna sell those rifles to the Mexican rebels, then that's fine. You can ride on through and we won't shoot!'

'It's a trick. You ride through there, they'll fire on you, I guarantee it!' urged Tate in desperation.

Chico's thin lips drew in a smile. 'Now it suits you to say that white men are treacherous, but your money has brought us only trouble.'

'Very well, but we must have a hostage. We will let him go once we are safe!' Chico called back.

Pike turned to one of his men. 'Go

get Silver and bring him here.'

'I don't like this, Sergeant,' said Callaghan. 'Those men attacked Maxwell and killed innocent people. Now you're letting them go!'

'We know who they are and they'll get what's comin' to 'em another time, but right now this is the best way o' doin' things.'

'I'm inclined to agree with the sheriff. This hardly seems like honourable conduct,' protested Gorman.

'Let me tell you somethin', Mister. The army's full of asshole officers gettin' their men shot to pieces cos they wanna act honourable and earn themselves a medal. Well, I had a field commission as a captain durin' the war before they busted me back down to sergeant, and I never lost a man I didn't have to!'

Silver was brought forward, his hands bound in front of him, as Pike finished speaking. The sergeant gestured with his rifle. 'You see them Apaches down there? You're gonna be their hostage for the next five minutes.'

Silver shook his head. 'Wait a minute. I don't trust Apaches one bit.'

Pike grinned back at him. 'Neither do I. That's why I'm sendin' you.'

'You can't make me go down there.'

Pike cocked his rifle. 'I wouldn't bet on that if I were you. Now move it!'

The gunman reluctantly began to climb down to the path below. Chico watched his approach with a smile of triumph, then fixed Tate with a hard stare. Another Apache reached across and removed the outlaw's gun from its holster. The saddle-bags of stolen money were then brought forward and loaded on to his horse.

'Go, Tate. You belong with them,' Chico told him.

'Wait a minute. We had a deal. I thought you were people of your word!'

The Apache shook his head. 'Your deal was with Aldo. It was a mistake. Now go!'

Tate turned his heavily laden horse

and trotted slowly along the path. As Silver walked past him toward the Apaches, the two men barely glanced at each other. Pike sent a couple of men down to escort the prisoner and his horse up to the top of the range. When they were safely back and Silver was with the Apaches he called back down to Chico that he and his men could start moving.

The soldiers then watched intently as Chico gestured for Silver to walk in front of his men, a rifle pointed at his back while they moved slowly along the path, alert for any signs of attack.

Gorman shook his head contemptuously. 'I can't believe you're just letting those savages go.'

'I dunno what you're so sore about. We got the money back and caught the man who stole it. Besides, it's government policy to support Juarez against the Emperor Maximilian, and when the Apaches sell those rifles they'll be doin' that for us.'

'I understand why you made the

decision, but I still don't like it,' said Callaghan.

'You're bound to feel that way after what happened to your town an' all, but it was Tate who put 'em up to it and, like I said, here he is.'

All eyes now turned to the prisoner who stood before them. 'I should like some time to question this man before we move out,' said Gorman.

Pike shrugged. 'Sure, let's just get this over with first.' Then he turned his attention back to the Apaches moving below as the last of them disappeared.

Meanwhile, Silver was feeling distinctly nervous. They had now emerged into the desert on the other side of the range, and he halted. The Apaches surrounded him in a circle and for a moment he thought they were going to attack. Then their leader gestured back toward the path. 'Go, the soldiers kept their word, so now we keep ours.'

Silver turned around and walked away slowly before he was stopped by a shout.

'Wait! You will answer one question before you leave.'

The gunman stopped and turned around. 'What do you want to know?'

'Is there a woman travelling with the soldiers?'

Silver affected a nonchalant shrug. 'I haven't seen one.'

Chico came closer and peered at him. 'I remember. You were one of the ones brought to her brother, Salinas. Aldo left you to die in the desert with Callaghan and the others, but she saved you.'

'Oh, you mean Christina. I thought you people captured her,' replied Silver, trying to sound surprised.

'She killed Aldo and fled. Then someone helped her, someone who killed two of my men.'

The gunman felt as if Chico's eyes were boring through him, drilling down into his very soul. 'I don't know anything about that. This is a big desert. She could be lost or dead along with whoever helped her.'

To his relief, the Apache nodded and gestured for him to be on his way, but Silver knew the other man's gaze was on his retreating back until he was out of sight.

Pike watched as Silver came back along the path. 'It looks like we can all relax. The Apaches have gone on their way.'

Gorman then stood up and hustled Tate away at gunpoint. 'Come on, I want some answers from you.'

When the two of them were sitting in a corner of one of the caves, Gorman started his interrogation. 'What were you thinking of, Tate? You were only supposed to steal the money, not massacre all those people and try to make it look like Indians did it!'

The outlaw shrugged. 'You sold the information in return for ten per cent of the cut. I don't recall you being so particular then about how I got my hands on the money.'

'Well, now you've really landed yourself in a pickle. Killing all those people means it won't just be jail time.'

'Aren't you forgetting something?'

'What's that?'

'If I go down, so do you. I can always tell where I got my information from, and if I add in a little white lie about you knowing exactly what I was going to do, that'll make you an accessory to murder.'

Gorman sat back, astonished. 'What good will that do you?'

'None, but it gives you a little incentive to find me a way out of this, preferably with the money.'

'How can I do that? It's far too dangerous. Besides, I think I can get Silver to turn state's evidence and put that fool Carver in the frame.'

Tate smiled and shook his head. 'Come on, if you've already talked to Silver you know he won't do that. He's suddenly discovered his conscience.'

'Having some conscience isn't a bad thing. I may be corrupt, but I couldn't have done what you did and kill all those people.'

'No, but you weren't too squeamish to let me do it for you,' said Tate with contempt. 'Anyway, this isn't getting us anywhere. Like I told you, find me a way out or it'll be as bad for you too. I'll see to that.'

Gorman's mind raced furiously. 'All right. Say nothing about where you got the information or point the finger at Carver or anybody you like except me. I'll get you out, before the trial if I can.'

'What about the money?'

Gorman shook his head. 'Look, get yourself to Mexico and hire some new men. I'll let you know when something big comes up and it will be the same deal as before, but no killings this time. Make sure you vanish afterwards, understood?'

Tate nodded. 'OK, it's a deal. I know how badly you want the money. Detectives get lousy pay.'

'Yes, bringing you in should get me some reward money but I mustn't be tied to your escape. That's why it's better if it happens when you're not in my custody.'

Tate nodded. 'I understand, but you know what will happen if you double cross me.'

Gorman nodded as he stood up. 'If I didn't know who I was dealing with before, I certainly do now.'

7

Chico was deep in thought as he rode off with his men. He did not recall seeing the fair-haired gunman among the townspeople at Maxwell. If he had been in jail, Callaghan would have left him there, surely? No, Silver must have escaped during the battle and been captured by the soldiers later. Could he have come across the Mexican girl? Whoever killed the two men he sent after her could shoot extremely well. His mind made up, he signalled his followers to halt and summoned his best scout. The man listened carefully to Chico's instructions, and then set off to follow the cavalry. When he returned, Chico would know the truth.

★   ★   ★

Meanwhile, Pike was feeling pleased with himself. 'We got the money back and captured two murderers without a shot bein' fired.'

'So what happens now?' asked Callaghan.

'We'll escort you and the young lady back to Maxwell, then take the prisoners on to Fort Bowie.'

'Tate and Silver should be placed in civil, not military custody,' protested Gorman. They may have stolen army money but they robbed a coach and killed civilians. This case is a federal matter.'

'Don't you ever quit with your damned complaints?' demanded Pike, sourly. 'I'll send for the county sheriff or a deputy from Tucson when we get to the fort.'

'I've got a better idea. I'll send a telegram from Maxwell, and someone should reach Fort Bowie by the time you get there,' suggested Callaghan.

The sergeant gave a grunt of approval. 'Good thinkin' Sheriff. The sooner I get those fellas outta my hair, the happier I'll be.'

Callaghan then turned to Gorman. 'Does that satisfy you?'

'Since there are only two prisoners, one other armed escort apart from myself should be sufficient.'

'You didn't turn up anything against Matt, did you?'

'No, your friend is free to go,' conceded the detective, 'for the present at least.'

Callaghan ignored the implied threat and turned to Christina as she drew up alongside him. 'I'm sorry you've been through such an ordeal. I'd give anything for none of it to have happened.'

She shook her head. 'I don't regret anything, Luke. I've taken control of my life for the first time.'

'When I first saw you, you were as much your brother's prisoner as I was, however much you tried to defy him. What changed?'

'Can't you guess?' She smiled at his

look of puzzlement. 'It was you, Luke. I saw your courage and your decency. I knew then that I had to do something.'

'Well, you saved my life.'

'And mine too,' added Carver from behind them. 'I'm very grateful, of course, and so's my Rosie. She says you and our gallant sheriff here would make the perfect couple.'

'Aw, cut it out Matt!' Callaghan flushed with embarrassment and turned away. 'Pay no attention to him, Christina. He's always trying to get me married off.'

She smiled mischievously at Carver. 'That sounded like a rejection, Matt. How soon do you think I'll get over it?'

Feigning more discomfort than he felt, Callaghan dismissed her remark with a shrug. 'You're as bad as he is with your teasing.' Her response secretly pleased him, however. She had not appeared to take the idea seriously, but neither had she dismissed it, and those brief imaginings he had entertained of a life with her now appeared

184

again, but this time they lingered in his mind.

★ ★ ★

The scout Chico had sent to spy on the column now emerged from his hiding place at the foot of a canyon behind some rocks and sagebrush. As the cavalry passed into the distance he turned back to report to his chief. It did not take him long to catch up with his companions, and the Apache leader listened intently as he reported what he had seen.

'We must avenge Aldo. His spirit will not rest until the girl and the man called Silver pay for what they have done!'

There was a murmur of agreement from his men before the whole group turned to follow the cavalry's trail. They moved swiftly and caught up with Pike and his men shortly after they had stopped for a rest. It was a sharp-eyed Christina who spotted them first.

'It looks like we have trouble approaching,' she warned the sergeant.

Pike watched the cloud of dust get closer before he made out the colourful clothing and painted faces of the Mescalero Apaches.

'They're about to attack!' cried a young cavalryman in fear.

'Keep calm, soldier!' Pike admonished him. 'If they were gonna do that we'd know about it by now. They'd be hollerin' those damned war cries louder than all the devils in hell.'

'This doesn't look good, though, does it?' asked Callaghan.

'Well, they want somethin' all right. Let's just wait and see what it is before we get too nervous.'

The Apaches drew closer, then slowed and drew to a halt. Chico rode forward as his men waited behind him. When he stopped, his eyes scanned the assembled men in their dusty uniforms and then settled on Christina. He pointed directly at her as he spoke.

'The woman who rides with you is

our enemy. She killed our chief.' His finger then moved and settled on the bound figure of Silver. 'He is the one who helped her. You will give them to us, then go your way.'

'I ain't givin' you nobody. We had a deal and I kept my side of it,' replied Pike with a show of defiance.

Chico shook his head. 'I did not know that she was among you or the fair-haired one who helped her.'

The sergeant shrugged. 'That don't make no difference. A deal's a deal, and now you wanna break your word, is that it?'

Chico stiffened in his saddle. 'I am Apache! We do not break our word as white men break treaties!'

Pike shook his head. 'Don't lay that one on me. We could've slaughtered you and all your men in that canyon, but we didn't. Now the odds are more in your favour it's a different story.'

'Not so. I give you the same chance to leave. We only kill if you refuse. Aldo wanted the woman for his wife. She killed him and ran away. Silver killed two of my men for her. They were not there to kill him. Now, for crimes against Apache, we want Apache justice!'

'Aldo tried to rape her and she defended herself. How is a slow and painful death in return for that justice?' demanded Callaghan.

'You let the woman go with Aldo to spare your own people,' Chico reminded him. 'Now, I give you one hour to decide. Then, you give up our enemies or we attack and kill you all!'

As Chico turned to go, Callaghan called out to him. 'You will not attack in less than an hour, even if we move from here. Do you swear it?'

The Apache gave him a thin smile. 'Flee if you wish. We will soon catch you, but yes, I swear not to attack within the hour.' Then he turned and rode back to his men.

'Damn it, we're in a real tight spot now!' said Pike.

'Not necessarily, Sergeant. I'll tell

them Silver is due to hang, and perhaps they'll be content with that.' Christina began to ride forward, but Callaghan seized her horse's bridle.

'For God's sake, stop it! Don't you realize what they'll do to you?'

When she turned to him, her features were stricken with fear. 'Of course I do, but what's my life worth when there are so many others at stake?'

'The lady does have a point,' suggested Gorman. 'Perhaps we could negotiate, persuade them to just shoot her . . . ' His voice trailed away as he found himself surrounded by hostile faces.

'You call yourself a detective, an officer of the law, and yet you suggest such a thing! How could you?' demanded Callaghan in disgust.

'Yeah, I wouldn't hand Silver over to 'em neither, 'cos there's such a thing as the law and the constitution of the United States,' added Pike. 'There's not a man here today who wouldn't rather die at the hands o' them Apaches than do such a thing.'

'Well, I have no intention of dying here,' protested Gorman. 'I shall make for Maxwell straightaway.'

He found himself staring down the barrel of Callaghan's revolver. 'You'll stand and fight with us or I swear to God I'll kill you myself!' The Wells Fargo detective sat trembling in his saddle but said nothing, seeing there was no point.

The sheriff then turned to Pike. 'Look, there's an escarpment over there, just a few hundred yards away. If we move to the top, they'll have a much harder job attacking us.'

'Yeah, we might just have a chance of holding 'em off. Come on, let's go!' He ordered his men to saddle up, and the column prepared to head for the slope.

'You don't have to come,' Callaghan told Christina. 'Ride to Maxwell and get the next stage to Tucson. You'll be safe there.'

She shook her head. 'It's no use, Luke. If you don't defeat them today, they'll catch me up. I'm better off taking my chances here, and I know how to shoot.' Her voice faltered as she added, 'I can save a bullet for myself if I have to.'

'It'll be all right,' he told her with more confidence than he felt.

It was a steep climb for both men and horses to the top of the escarpment, and they found themselves slipping as loose stones and rocks were dislodged on the way up. At last they reached the ridge at the top, and Pike strung his men along it.

'How about letting me fight?' Silver raised his bound hands. 'You need all the help you can get, and a hangman's noose is better than what they'll do to me.'

'How do I know you won't try to make a run for it?' demanded the sergeant.

Silver shrugged. 'I don't reckon it would do me much good.'

'No, I don't reckon it would,' agreed Pike as he cut the man's bonds.

He then looked hesitantly at Tate. 'Now you, I really don't trust at all. If I see you even look like you're gonna run, I'll shoot you down, Apaches or no Apaches. Is that understood?'

The outlaw nodded in response as his hands were freed, and then Pike ordered that Tate and Silver be issued with arms. Gorman opened his mouth to protest, but then thought better of it. After all, he was more reluctant to die than any of them.

Chico was now regretting his decision to give Pike and his men so much time. Still, a worthy opponent was more satisfying to defeat than a weak and cowardly one. He glanced down at the gold pocket watch he had taken from an officer he had killed. The one thing he recalled clearly from his brief spell at school on the reservation was being taught to tell the time. This knowledge was to prove useful occasionally. Snapping the lid shut, he signalled his men to attack and they began to move. Leaving the horses behind, they crept forward on foot, as it was easier to climb that way.

The men at the top of the escarpment unleashed a torrent of gunfire and the dead bodies of Chico's warriors began to fall back down the slope as if flung by an invisible giant. Their companions crouched lower to evade the hail of bullets. Some lay flat or hid behind the boulders scattered along the way as they fired back. The air was now thick with smoke, and the only sounds apart from gunfire were the cries of dying men as some of the return fire began to hit home. The foot of the escarpment was just out of range and Chico ordered some of his followers to move around to the right and then climb up the other side behind Pike's men.

'Damn sneaky Indians!' shouted the sergeant as he spotted the move and ordered some of his men to turn around and start shooting the other way. They managed to pick off those leading this rearguard attack, and the others wisely fell back in an orderly retreat.

'They'll be back,' warned Callaghan as he shot a young warrior in the face at point-blank range and watched his body tumble down the escarpment. Their opponents were getting perilously close now and some of the soldiers were having to stand and engage in hand-to-hand combat as their enemies threatened to overwhelm them. With no time to reload if a man ran out of bullets, rifles were used as clubs to smash against bones and drive their assailants back. Callaghan spotted one soldier taking on two men at once, each armed with a tomahawk. Rushing to help, the lawman shot one in the stomach with his last bullet and then rammed the butt of his rifle under the other attacker's chin with a blow that lifted the Apache off his feet and sent him flying. A third warrior then leaped at him, his dagger raised. The sheriff rolled on to his side and fired, hitting the knifeman in the neck with a shot that choked off his war cry.

As Callaghan turned back an Apache loomed over him and raised a rifle to bring the butt crashing down on his skull. He squeezed the trigger on his revolver once more and heard only the click of an empty chamber, then moved aside just in time to avoid a fatal blow. The sheriff then leaped to his feet and pistol-whipped his attacker around the face and head, frantically lashing out to drive the man away. Blood gushed from the Apache's nose and forehead as his body crumpled, and a final kick in the chest sent him falling backwards.

Another warrior appeared in his place, his painted face contorted with rage, but a shot suddenly ripped through his chest, and the Apache looked down in apparent disbelief at the stain that now spread across his brightly coloured shirt. Callaghan turned around to see that Silver had been his protector, and gave the gunman a brief nod of thanks. Gorman and Tate were both further back, firing from a distance at those few Apaches who managed to break through. This was useful but somewhat safer than being in the front line, and Pike snarled at them to move further forward.

At that moment, Chico ordered his men to retreat and there was a muted cheer from Pike's men as the Apaches fell back.

'Don't get your hopes up. They'll be back soon enough,' growled the battle-worn sergeant who had witnessed this tactic before.

'What do you think of our chances?' asked Callaghan as both men reloaded their weapons.

'I reckon we lost over twenty men and got barely a dozen o' theirs. They'll attack from both sides again once they've regrouped, and this time it'll be harder to hold 'em off.'

'We need a distraction, something to draw enough of them away to give us a chance.'

'You got any ideas?'

The sheriff pointed to a waggon standing at a safe distance from the fighting. 'That's got the weapons from their hideout on it. It looks to me like there are a couple of kegs on board.'

Pike peered through his spyglass. 'Yeah, they got some powder on there all right. What about it?'

'There are still horses tethered to it. If a couple of men could get down there and drive it away, some of the Apaches would come after it. The fuse would need to be timed right for them to catch up, the men could jump clear and then . . . '

'Boom! It's a damned crazy idea, so crazy it might just work. Who's gonna do it?'

'I thought of it, so I guess I ought to go. Silver's quite agile so I'll take him.'

'Yeah, agile and expendable, which you ain't — expendable, I mean. Why don't you let me send one of my men with him?'

Callaghan shook his head. 'Your men have risked their lives enough already.

All this has come about because of choices I made. It's up to me to finish it.'

'I understand. We'll try to cover you as best we can. Good luck.' The two men shook hands and the sheriff went to give Silver his instructions. The gunman listened carefully and then nodded his assent when Callaghan finished.

'I was expecting some kind of objection.'

'Would it do any good?'

'No, I figure it's the least you could do, even though you saved my life back there.'

Silver shrugged. 'I guess you're right. Besides, I'm a condemned man with a lot of paying back to do.'

'Then let's get started.'

As the two men rose to go, Christina approached them. 'What's this I hear, Luke? Have you gone completely mad?'

'It's the only way. We'll all be massacred otherwise.'

'But why does it have to be you? Let

someone else go. What about Tate? This is all his fault after all!'

'Do you trust him? Tate would only try to make a run for it, or kill me and give himself up to Chico, selling us all out in exchange for his life.'

'I know you're right. It just all seems so unfair . . . ' Her voice trailed away and she shrugged helplessly.

'I'll be back, don't worry.' Callaghan gave her a reassuring smile as he turned away. Silver followed behind and Christina seized his arm.

'Try to keep him safe, please.'

The gunman looked in to her eyes for a moment, then gently released her grip. 'I'll do my best,' he told her.

The two men made their way to the far edge of the escarpment and climbed down as Chico launched his next attack. The Apaches were some distance to the left of them and focused on their assault; none of them spotted Callaghan and Silver until they had reached the foot of the slope and were running across the desert plain towards the waggon. Then one of Chico's men happened to look down and saw them. Turning, he pointed his rifle at the two figures below and fired. The shot landed barely an inch from Callaghan, whizzing past his ear. The two men began to zig zag as other warriors fired at them too, the bullets throwing up clouds of dust as they landed all around them. At last they reached the waggon and Silver threw himself in the back as Callaghan lashed the horses into a fury.

By now Chico had sent some of his men after them in pursuit. They ran back down the slope, leaped on to their waiting horses and set off at a gallop after the two men and their stolen weapons. Silver busied himself with the fuses, tying one to each of the powder kegs while keeping an eye on their rapidly approaching pursuers.

'They're gaining on us already!' he cried as he picked off the two nearest the front with his revolver.

'Then get those damned fuses lit. We

haven't much time!' Callaghan called back.

Silver fumbled for his matches as another Apache came to the front, leaped from his mount and landed in the back of the waggon. The outlaw snatched up his gun and fired just in time. He struck a match and lit the first fuse as the Apache's body fell under the wheels.

'Can't you go any faster? I'm not ready yet!' he pleaded.

Callaghan lashed the horses once again, urging them on and they began to pull away as Silver lit the second fuse. The gunman heard a thud as another warrior climbed on to the top of the waggon and ripped the cloth covering with his knife. He fired upwards through the slit and the dead man tumbled through the opening, landing on top of his assailant's legs. The corpse was heavy and Silver struggled to free himself as the fuses burned down.

'Hey, slow a little and then jump. I'll follow!'

Callaghan pulled on the reins and felt the sweating horses slacken their pace, allowing the Apaches to catch up once more. Then he leaped and rolled over as he hit the ground. Winded, he stumbled to his feet just in time to see the shrieking warriors surround the waggon. There was no sign of Silver, however.

The trapped gunman gave a smile of satisfaction as his tormentors swarmed over the vehicle. The fuses had almost burned down but there was no point in waiting. One of them might notice in time to put them out.

'Take a short ride to hell!' cried Silver as he fired his last bullet at the keg nearest him.

The sound of the explosion was deafening when it came, accompanied by blinding flashes and orange flames that leaped up high into the air. A series of smaller explosions followed as crates of ammunition and a small box containing sticks of nitroglycerine went off. Every pursuing Apache was caught in the blast, and those who had been on the waggon were the most fortunate as they were killed outright. Those who had been at the rear lay scattered around as burnt and bloodied vestiges of the men they had once been. Callaghan walked among these heaps of torn clothes and scorched flesh, dispensing a bullet where he heard feeble cries that indicated a man was still alive enough to feel pain. It was the horses he pitied most, however, for they were innocent and he attended to them first.

Then he made his way back to the main battle. As he approached he saw that Chico and his depleted force were being driven back. The sound of the explosion and the loss of both their companions and their valuable cargo had disheartened the enemy. Pike lost no time in pressing home his advantage. His men had mounted their horses and were riding down the slope after the fleeing Apaches, whom they now outnumbered.

Callaghan edged his way further up towards the mêlée. As he did so, he saw the intrepid Chico dodge a blow from a pursuing cavalryman, then drag the soldier from his horse and club him over the head. The Apache then leaped nimbly into the saddle and began to ride away. The sheriff pulled his gun and fired but it was an awkward shot from that angle amid the fleeing horde of warriors. The horse crumpled beneath its rider and Chico was thrown to the ground. Knowing he had used his last bullet, Callaghan swore with frustration and flung the weapon at him but Chico jumped aside and drew his knife.

The lawman was unarmed, and could only retreat as the blade swung towards him, narrowly avoiding a slit throat as he did so. Chico moved in again with a stabbing motion aimed at his heart and Callaghan turned sideways. His opponent had over-reached himself and he seized the Apache's wrist, twisting it as he did so. The weapon dropped from his numbed fingers, but he moved in closer and tripped Callaghan as he did so. The sheriff now hit the ground with his adversary on top of him. The Apache's hands reached for his throat and pressed down hard. Callaghan bucked and squirmed, his hands clawing at the man's arms in a desperate attempt to loosen his opponent's grip. It was no use, and he felt his struggles grow weaker as his lungs were starved of air. Then he felt something beneath him: it was the knife Chico had dropped. Summoning what remained of his strength, he thrust it into the Apache's side, and the man's grip immediately loosened. Callaghan withdrew the blade, then rolled aside and staggered to his feet.

Chico grunted in pain as he clutched the wound, blood seeping between his fingers. It was by no means fatal, but the sheriff had the advantage now, and it was he who retreated as Callaghan moved towards him. Crouching down, he picked up a fistful of sand and tossed it in the white man's face. The sheriff was momentarily blinded and felt a shape move towards him, his eyes stinging. The Apache flung himself at his enemy with a cry but misjudged the move. Callaghan kept a good grip on the knife and it was pointed upwards as Chico threw him to the ground. The blade ripped through the warrior's lungs and he gave a choked cry, blood frothing from his lips. It took a moment for the sheriff to realize what had happened, but then he shoved the dead man's body aside and stumbled once more to his feet. The few remaining Apaches had fled, and the exhausted cavalrymen now ceased their pursuit. It was over.

Pike slowed his horse and stopped beside him. 'Well, I gotta hand it you. It worked.'

'Yeah, I told you it would.'

'By the way, where's Silver?'

Callaghan shook his head. 'He didn't make it.'

The sergeant shrugged. 'Well, I reckon it was better than hanging.'

Christina then ran towards them and

a moment later she was in Callaghan's arms.

'I guess I'll just leave you to it,' added Pike as he rode off.

'I was so afraid you wouldn't come back.' She cupped the sheriff's face in her hands, her eyes scanning him through her tears for signs of injury.

'I'm fine, but Silver didn't get out of the waggon in time.'

'He wasn't all bad, Luke, despite the things he did.'

'No. In different circumstances, if he'd taken a different path maybe, he might even have been a lawman.'

She took his hand in hers. 'Let's go join the others. It looks like the worst is over.'

At that moment Carver came running towards them, Gorman hard on his heels. 'Tate's gone, Luke. Have you seen him?'

'No. How did he get away?'

'That's what I'd like to know. I warned Pike against giving him a gun!' Gorman appeared flushed with anger, or perhaps it was just the effort of running.

'He must have stolen a horse and slipped away during the cavalry charge,' said Carver.

'Well then, let's not panic. He can't have got far, and we know he must be heading for the border.'

'There's no sense the whole troop chasing him. This man is my responsibility and I'll catch him,' said Gorman imperiously.

'He's desperate, and that makes him even more dangerous,' urged Callaghan. 'Matt and I will go with you.'

'Well, if you insist, though I assure you there's no need,' conceded the detective.

'You need to rest, Luke. Haven't you done enough for one day?' pleaded Christina.

'Miss Salinas is right, Sheriff. It was a very brave thing you did earlier. Perhaps it's time you let others take the risks.'

'Thanks, I appreciate that.' Callaghan

was surprised by this act of conciliation from the prickly detective. 'Nevertheless, I was the first to suspect Tate and apprehend him, so I feel obliged to help.'

Christina gave a sigh of resignation and shot Carver a pleading look. 'Watch out for this stubborn man.'

Carver nodded. 'Don't worry,' he told her.

'Come on, let's get our horses. There's no time to waste,' said Gorman, suddenly imperious again.

In no time at all the three men had mounted up, and they quickly found the fugitive's trail. They set a steady pace. Tate would be expecting pursuers, but could not risk wearing out or injuring his horse in the desert heat, and neither could they.

They were approaching the range where they had spent the previous night when Carver spotted a figure riding ahead of them. 'It must be him. Look, this trail's fresh.'

'Excuse me, gentlemen, but this is

my fight.' Gorman dug his spurs into his horse's side and set off at a gallop.

'That man's a damned fool!' declared Callaghan.

'I figure he wants the glory of recapturing Tate all for himself,' said Carver. 'But I guess we'd better go help.'

The pair raced after him but the detective was now far ahead of them. By the time they reached the foot of the range, there were two horses tethered to a bush by the narrow path, and no sign of either man.

'Tate must be armed. He probably figured it was best to reach a vantage point up there and pick us off. Leaving his horse behind was a smart move, he can move quicker that way,' remarked Callaghan.

'I guess Gorman didn't want to be a sitting duck, and neither do we.' Carver dismounted and drew his gun. Callaghan did the same. The two men then began a cautious climb upwards.

8

Gorman moved quickly up the path, ignoring his aching limbs and the sweat that poured off him. He could see Tate up ahead and ducked down behind a boulder as the outlaw turned and fired a shot in his direction.

'Stop! It's me, Gorman! You haven't got a chance!' he called after him.

'I'm not going back!' replied Tate as he turned in panic and let off two more shots. Gorman threw himself back behind the boulder as the first one whizzed past his ear and the second bullet ricocheted off the ground. Then he heard the click of an empty chamber and came out from his hiding place, his gun pointed straight at Tate's chest.

'We've got a deal. You can't take me back!'

The detective smiled as he walked towards him. 'No, Tate. You're right, I can't take you back. You'd talk, wouldn't you?'

'So, you let me go and we'll get another job organized, right?'

Still smiling and pointing the gun, Gorman shook his head.

The sudden realization of his accomplice's real intent came too late. 'Now, hold on a minute . . .'

Tate's last words were cut off in midsentence as Gorman fired three shots at point-blank range. The outlaw slumped sideways, crumpled to the ground and lay still. Gorman approached the dead man cautiously, still pointing his gun. He gave Tate a shove with his foot and was relieved to hear no moaning sounds or signs of breathing. Blood pooled beneath the body as Callaghan and Carver arrived, both men panting heavily.

'I tried to take him alive but he fired at me twice,' said Gorman.

The sheriff bent down and picked up the dead man's revolver. His eyes widened in surprise when he opened the chamber. 'Well, they were his last two bullets.'

The detective shrugged. 'I didn't know that. I guess he didn't either since he made no attempt to surrender.'

'Maybe he preferred it this way, to hanging I mean,' suggested Carver.

'That doesn't sound like Tate to me. I'd expect him to be trying to figure a way out even as he stepped on to the gallows,' replied Callaghan.

'I mean no disrespect, but I expect you have little experience of desperate outlaws like Tate. The manner of his death was entirely in keeping with the way he lived, I assure you,' said Gorman.

'Even so, I thought you'd be disappointed that he couldn't be taken alive.'

Gorman shrugged. 'Oh, I know he's escaped the noose, but if a man gets hanged properly he should die straightaway from a broken neck. I don't see the difference, really.'

'I was thinking more of the mystery

you haven't solved. With Tate dead, how will you ever find out who gave him his information?'

'Well, when I questioned Silver, he seemed to think that it was from either the guard or the driver. Tate was certainly ruthless enough to double cross an accomplice.' He nodded in Carver's direction. 'I have concluded that Mister Carver here knew nothing of it. My apologies for suggesting otherwise.'

'Forget it. I guess you were just doing your job,' said the station agent.

'It's good of you to be so understanding. Well, gentlemen. I suggest we bury Tate out here and re-join Sergeant Pike and his men.'

When they finally caught up with Pike and his men, the sergeant asked them what happened.

'Mister Gorman here shot our fugitive,' explained Callaghan.

'Apparently, Tate was more desperate than we thought, and didn't surrender even when he had no bullets left.'

Pike raised his eyebrows. 'Is that a fact? Well, I guess it's no loss. I got better things to do than drag some outlaw's ass across the desert.'

'You must be relieved this business is all over,' said Carver.

'Yeah, I guess I am. Now I just wanna get these exhausted men and the payroll money to Fort Bowie.'

'You're welcome to rest up at Maxwell for a day or two,' Callaghan told him. 'It's the least we can do after all you've done.'

'Well, there's a lotta men here. We wouldn't want to be any trouble. Soldiers ain't the easiest guests to have,' said Pike reluctantly.

'It'd be no trouble. We can put some of them up at the inn, and folks will be glad to billet others in their houses,' Carver urged him.

Pike's bearded features broke in to a grin. 'Well, in that case we'll be glad to accept your invitation.'

'What about you? You'll be in no hurry now you've no prisoners to

215

escort,' Callaghan asked Gorman.

'Thank you, Sheriff. I'd be glad of a rest. It would be convenient, as I do have other business to attend to in Tucson and can get the stage from Maxwell.'

Their journey now continued without incident. 'Why did you invite that snake Gorman to stay in town?' grumbled Carver as they prepared to make camp at dusk.

'It seemed impolite not to since he's travelling with Pike's men. Besides, it gives me a chance to watch him.'

'What for?'

Callaghan shook his head. 'I don't know, but he's hiding some secret. There's something odd about the way he went after Tate, not like him at all.'

'I see what you mean,' conceded the station agent. 'He's not exactly brave, is he? Yet he seemed to forget all about the danger this afternoon. It was almost as if he had to kill Tate.'

'That's what I figured. And why was he so keen to pin you down as an accessory? He seems to have forgotten all about that now.'

'Well, whatever it is, we'll just have to keep an eye on him and hope he makes a mistake.'

Callaghan nodded slowly. 'Oh, that's one thing people who break the law always do eventually.'

Dusk was falling and the weary travellers had endured a long day of dust and sweat with a hard battle thrown in. They made camp for the night and Callaghan fell into a deep and dreamless slumber. The sun was up and men were bustling around him when he finally awoke and sat up groggily. Carver handed him steaming coffee in a tin cup and a plate of beans.

'The breakfast's a bit basic. I think Pike might be getting low on supplies.'

'Anything would taste good this morning. Yesterday I wasn't sure I'd ever see the sun come up again.'

'Me neither, but we did.' Both men spied Christina tending to her horse a short distance away. 'So, are you gonna marry that girl or what?' the station agent asked.

'Cut it out, Matt.' Callaghan's face reddened as he shovelled a spoonful of beans into his mouth. 'I've got other things to think about right now.'

'Like what?'

'What we were talking about yesterday.'

'Oh, Gorman. What about it?'

'I reckon it was Gorman who gave Tate his tip-off about the payroll.'

Carver frowned. 'How do you figure that?

'Think about it. First, he was desperate to pin it on you — he even tried to get Silver to say it was you. Then, when all the outlaws were dead except the one man who knew the truth, what did he do?'

'He killed him,' said Carver, nodding slowly. 'When you put it like that it all makes sense — but you can't prove anything.'

Callaghan washed down the last of the beans with the dregs of his coffee cup. 'Maybe, maybe not. Anyway, there's something I could try that might just trap him, but I'll need Pike's help to make it work.'

'You still haven't answered my question.'

The sheriff stood up. 'No, I haven't, have I?' he replied with a grin.

'Well, you'd be crazy not to!' his friend called after his retreating back.

When they set off that morning, Callaghan rode at the front beside Pike. He confided his suspicions about Gorman during a whispered conversation, and the sergeant listened intently.

'Well, what do you think? I've tried to set aside the fact that I don't like the man, but it all seems very suspicious to me.'

'I reckon you're right, Sheriff. Gorman's gotta yellow streak and he was hardly winnin' medals against them Apaches. Then, suddenly, he's riskin' his neck to finish off Tate. It don't make no sense to me neither.'

'Then you'll help?'

'Sure I will. Just tell me what you want me to do.'

Callaghan outlined his plan, the sergeant nodding as he listened before giving a final grunt of approval.

'Well, I'm just a simple soldier but it sounds pretty good to me. Let's just hope it works.'

'If it doesn't, I'll have misjudged the man, but there'll be no harm done.'

The day's ride passed without incident until Maxwell finally came within sight. They heard the church bell being rung as they approached, and Callaghan was surprised to discover how quickly the townspeople had set about repairing the damage done by Aldo and his men. There was a smell of fresh paint in the air, and few signs of the carnage wrought only days previously, apart from the scorched areas of ground where the barrier had been burned down.

People gathered around Callaghan and the others as they rode along the main street, finally forcing them to a halt as they fired off questions about the events of the last few days.

'I don't see no prisoners, Sheriff. What happened to that varmint Tate? Did you shoot him?' one man called out.

'Mister Gorman here shot him,' Callaghan answered. All eyes turned to the detective and a cheer went up before more questions were fired at them.

'Come on now, folks, one at a time!' cried the sheriff, raising his hands to calm the crowd. 'You'll get all the answers you want in time, but the main things are we rescued Miss Salinas, defeated the Apaches and got the money back. Aldo, most of his men and all the outlaws are dead.'

'All right folks, you heard the sheriff!' called out Pike. 'Now, how about lettin' us all get some rest?'

At that moment Samuel Endicott stepped forward. 'I believe I speak for the whole town, Sergeant when I say that you and all your men can rest after you've eaten our food and danced to our music. This is a great day and we're going to celebrate!'

A great cheer went up and Callaghan, Pike and the others found themselves lifted from their horses by the exuberant crowd and carried shoulder high through the streets of Maxwell. Carver was the first to be set down, into the waiting arms of a weeping Rosie and young Stevie who beamed with pride.

There wasn't enough room to accommodate everyone in one building, so the feast that evening was held in the street. Tables laden with homemade pies, joints of meat and freshly baked bread were set out. People brought oil lamps from their homes to light up the darkening skies. The town boasted a fiddler, a harmonica player and a guitarist among its inhabitants, and if the music wasn't quite pitch perfect, it was at least lively, with tunes that set everyone's feet tapping.

'I've stashed the payroll money in the post office and put a couple of guards on the door outside,' Pike shouted to Gorman above the din.

'That sounds like a sensible arrangement. You have to be careful with such a large sum.'

'Yeah, that's what I figured — but somethin' bothers me.'

'What's that?' asked the detective.

The sergeant gestured expansively with his arm. 'These are good men, but the army's a hard life. You fight Indians and eat dust for a few dollars a day. If you're lucky you might live to draw an army pension, maybe even get some stripes on your arm. That money's a big temptation for these fellas, and more than a few of 'em know how to pick locks.'

Gorman leaned forward. 'Do you suspect anyone in particular, Sergeant?'

Pike shrugged. 'These are tough men, good in a fight but when it comes to thousands o' dollars, I'm not sure I'd trust any of 'em, to tell ya the truth Mister Gorman.'

Gorman nodded thoughtfully. 'I see

your problem. Is there any way I can help?'

Pike clamped him on the shoulder. 'I was kinda hopin' you'd ask that. I know we've had our differences, but I figure you to be honest, bein' a detective and a stickler for the rules an' all. Listen, I'd like you to take special charge o' that money. Hell, it ain't even been counted since it was stolen, so we don't know how much is there.'

'Is that so? Do you think some of it has gone missing already?' asked the detective with obvious interest.

'Well, it stands to reason, don't it? I mean, it's changed hands several times between Tate, Salinas and the Apaches. I'd be surprised if the full fifty thousand dollars was still there.'

'So what exactly do you want me to do?'

'Well, count it to start with. Then go back and count it a few more times over the next few days. Let me know if you find any missing and I'll take it from there. I'd do it myself, but I got my work cut out keepin' an eye on these men as it is. I can't ask the sheriff as he's rather preoccupied with that girl o' his.'

Gorman glanced over to see Christina and Callaghan dancing closely together. 'Yes, I see what you mean. Well, it's a simple task, Sergeant. Of course, I'd be happy to oblige.'

'That's great, a real weight off my mind. Now, here's a spare key to the front door and one to the safe. I know there's a party goin' on but I wonder if you'd mind makin' a start tonight?'

Gorman gave him a sly smile as he took the key. 'Not at all, Sergeant. Anything to set your mind at rest.'

Moments after Gorman had slipped out of his seat and headed to the post office, Callaghan made his excuses and returned to the table. Pike met his look of inquiry with a grin.

'I reckon we just gave our friend all the rope he needs. When I said that I didn't know how much money there was and some of it had probably been taken already, well you should ha' seen the look in those rat's eyes o' his!'

'So, now we wait,' replied Callaghan.

'Yeah, sit down and have a drink my friend. It's gonna be an interestin' night.'

Gorman strode confidently up the steps to the post office. The two men on duty outside barely glanced at him as he let himself in. Presumably Pike had told them to expect his arrival. He lit an oil lamp and a sickly yellow light illuminated the interior. The detective's tongue shot across his thin lips and he shivered with anticipation. He bent down, hands shaking and unlocked the door of the safe. The heavy iron door swung open and he dragged the saddle-bags of money over to the counter before methodically counting the contents of each one. He was surprised to find that the total came to fifty thousand dollars. Then he smiled to himself, realizing that Pike's mis-judgement allowed him to take a bigger share than he had intended.

Gorman then removed his jacket and carefully slit the lining open before removing it entirely. Taking bundles of notes from each bag, he laid them out in a thin layer, using only the largest denominations until a total of ten thousand dollars was reached, twice the cut promised by the late and unlamented Tate. Still, he reckoned the money had been well earned after all that chasing through the desert and fighting Apaches. He carefully placed the cash in an even layer inside the jacket and began the laborious process of stitching the lining back over it. This was going to take some time, but with the party in full swing, he knew he was not going to be disturbed. He worked quickly, his neck and shoulders aching as he bent over the cloth in the dim light. At last the final stitch was in place, and he put the jacket back on. There was a slight rustle if he ran his hand over the lining and it felt a little heavy to wear. However, there was no reason why anyone should notice

227

anything untoward, and it was much less risky than hiding it in his saddle-bag. All in all, he felt quite pleased with himself, especially since there was still time for him to rejoin the celebrations.

At that moment he was startled by a sudden creaking sound followed by a sharp intake of breath. Pulling his gun from its holster, he swung around to where the noise had come from. In the shadows, he could just make out the large storage cupboard in the corner of the room and the set of fingers around the edge of the door, pulling it closed after it had swung open. Gorman fired wildly in a blind panic. A witness was the one thing he could not afford. Four shots ripped through the mahogany door and it swung out once more. A small, crumpled figure slid out on to the floor, the dead eyes staring up sightlessly from behind a pair of wire-framed spectacles. Gorman recognized the face of Arthur Norris. What was that damned midget doing hiding in here, anyway?

The two guards burst in, rifles at the ready. They stared down at the dead man, then looked at each other, nonplussed.

'It's all right men. I've just caught a thief, that's all. He was hiding in that cupboard, waiting for a chance to steal this money.' Gorman spoke firmly, no sign of a tremor in his voice. The important thing was to get his story straight and stick to it.

'The man you shot appears to have been unarmed, Mister Gorman,' one of the men told him.

'Well, it's dark in here and I thought he had a weapon. When a thief jumps out on a man in the dark, what's he supposed to do?' demanded the detective with a show of belligerence.

At that moment, Callaghan and Pike burst in, having heard the shots from their table. The sheriff dropped down on one knee beside his friend, removed the spectacles and gently closed the dead man's eyes.

'He jumped out on me while I was counting the money, the wretched little thief. It was dark and I thought he had a gun,' said Gorman.

Callaghan looked up and stared hard at the detective. 'Arthur Norris was no thief. He wasn't here to steal that money, as I'm sure you realize. He was here to find out how much of it you were willing to take.'

'That's an outrageous suggestion! I counted forty thousand dollars and it's all here. You won't find a dollar missing, I assure you.' Gorman was sweating and trembling, his swivel-eyed glance moving from one man to another as he gripped his revolver.

'Forty thousand, eh? That's funny, Gorman, because when I counted it there was fifty thousand there,' Pike told him.

'But you said . . . '

'I know what I said, Gorman. I just wanted to see if you'd take the bait.'

'I see, so it was all a trick, was it? Well, your stupidity has cost a man his life and proved nothing. Go on, search me. Turn out my pockets and see what you find!'

Callaghan and Pike exchanged puzzled glances. The sergeant nodded to the guards. 'Go on, do what the man says.'

Gorman put his gun down and extended his arms. The two cavalrymen rifled through his pockets, tossing items on to the counter, but there were no bundles of notes. Besides, ten thousand dollars was an unusually large sum to hide that way.

'Has he been in here the whole time?' Pike asked.

Both soldiers nodded in response. Clearly the money was not going to be found in the detective's saddle-bag.

It was then that Callaghan noticed something. He picked up the reel of black cotton from among the contents of Gorman's pockets and looked at it curiously.

'What's this?' he asked, holding it up.

Gorman shrugged. 'Clothes get torn sometimes and need repairing.'

'It matches that jacket you're wearing. Take it off.'

'I will not suffer this indignity a moment longer!' Gorman began to stride toward the door, but Pike gave the guards a nod and they seized the detective before forcibly removing his jacket. One of them tossed the garment over to Callaghan, who quickly ripped the lining apart and emptied out the contents.

'That proves you're a thief as well as a murderer,' said the sheriff.

Gorman looked desperately from one man to another. 'All right, so I took some of the money but I'm no murderer. I thought there was an intruder . . .'

'I think you mean a witness,' said Callaghan, interrupting him.

'That's not all. I'm now certain that you sold Tate the information he needed to rob the right stage,' added Pike.

'That makes sense,' agreed Callaghan.

'It makes no sense at all!' protested Gorman. 'You have absolutely no proof for that assertion whatsoever!'

'It's mostly circumstantial,' conceded the sergeant. 'You tried to pin the blame on Carver and to persuade Silver to testify to that effect, but there's a clincher.'

The detective looked uncertain. 'You're bluffing!' he scoffed.

Pike shook his head. 'No, Gorman, your employer has suspected you for some time, so a little trap was laid and you've fallen right into it.'

'I don't understand,' said Callaghan.

'It's quite simple. All the money on that Wells Fargo stage was fake. The real payroll had already been delivered on the previous one, but Gorman didn't know that. In fact, he was the only Wells Fargo detective who didn't know the truth. Even the men carrying it knew the money wasn't real. They were all sworn to secrecy.'

Callaghan suddenly exploded with anger. 'That means that all the people on that stage died for nothing! The people of this town died defending nothing!' He grabbed a wad of notes and ripped them to shreds.

'Take it easy, Sheriff. We had no way of knowing what would happen. There'd been other robberies of large sums and Wells Fargo suspected information was being sold by one of their operatives. Previously no one had been hurt, but Tate obviously decided to do things differently.'

'Look, this is all a mistake. I just stole some money, after a lot of temptation was put in my way,' said Gorman.

'If that's your defence, it won't stand up in court,' Pike told him. 'You're an accessory to the murder of those folks on that stage since it can be proved you must have given that information to Tate.'

'To hell with being an accessory!' shouted Callaghan. 'He killed Arthur Norris in cold blood and he'll hang for it here in this town!'

'Sure, that can be added to the other

charges and it's the easiest one to prove,' conceded the sergeant. He turned to the two guards restraining the dejected Gorman. 'Take him to the jail.'

Callaghan stepped forward and drew his revolver. 'This is my town, Pike, and he committed murder here. I'll put him in jail myself.' Pulling Gorman roughly by the arm, he shoved him through the door at gunpoint and marched him down the street toward the jail.

Minutes later, the sheriff was locking the cell door as the disgraced detective peered at him through the bars.

'Look, Pike put me up to stealing that money, but I didn't know your friend was there. I thought . . .'

'Tell it to the jury, Gorman. They won't believe you any more than I do.'

When the lawman came outside, he found Pike waiting for him. 'I'll post a man in there to guard him if you like,' he suggested.

'Thanks, I can't stand to look at the weasel.' Callaghan's response was curt.

'Look, I can understand why you're

sore at me, but what I said earlier was true. There was no way to predict that massacre or the things that happened later. I can't tell you how sorry I am.'

Somewhat mollified by this admission, Callaghan asked, 'Where do you fit in to all this?'

'During the war I worked for Alan Pinkerton. I did secret stuff like gettin' disguised as a confederate and goin' behind enemy lines to find information, that kinda thing.'

'You mean you were some sort of spy.'

Pike shrugged. 'Yeah, I guess you could call it that. Anyway, with my record bein' known to my superiors, I got drafted in after this payroll thing started. When Wells Fargo got hired to carry it, they admitted they were havin' problems when there was a really big consignment o' cash bein' carried. They suspected one of their detectives was sellin' 'em out to outlaws for a cut.'

'And you helped them narrow down

the list of suspects and lay a trap, I suppose.'

The sergeant nodded. 'That's right, only now I wish I hadn't.'

Callaghan shook his head. 'It wasn't your fault. Besides, Gorman would have gone on doing it and people often get killed when stagecoaches are robbed. He might have ended up with even more blood on his hands.'

'I doubt he could have caused more deaths than there've been these last few days. Still, I'm glad you can see it that way.'

'I guess I'd better tell people about what happened. Nobody else heard the shots.'

Pike placed a hand on his shoulder. 'Leave it until mornin'. Folks are havin' a good time. Let 'em all mourn tomorrow when we bury your friend.'

'I reckon that's good advice. I'll just come say goodnight to Christina, then I guess I'll turn in.'

When he saw Christina, she looked anxiously at his troubled expression, searching his face for clues about what had happened.

'What is it, Luke? Please tell me.'

Callaghan shook his head. 'There's some bad news, but it can wait until morning. For now, how about one last dance?'

As they danced with the other couples and he felt her close to him, he let the events of the last hour slip from his mind for a few precious moments.

'Shall I stay with your tonight?' she whispered. 'Whatever's happened, let me help you to forget it until tomorrow.'

'When I'm with you, I forget everything else anyway,' he admitted. It proved to be true throughout the night that followed, but as the sun rose and she slept silently beside him, Callaghan knew that the bitter truth of his friend's death could no longer be kept a secret.

The Reverend Samuel Endicott led the funeral service, extolling the virtues of their departed friend, especially his deep love of Maxwell and his faith in its future. 'If we wish to honour Arthur's memory, then we must continue to rebuild our town and let it grow, providing a warm welcome for all who wish to make their home among us.'

Callaghan was one of the pallbearers when the coffin was carried outside the church and lowered into the earth. He could not bear to watch as the soil was thrown over it, turning to walk away from the huddle of mourners.

'It wasn't your fault, Luke. Arthur was very keen to help when you asked him to be your lookout, and he was the only man in the town small enough to fit in that cupboard,' Pike told him. Then he handed him a telegram.

'It's a reply to one I sent last night,' the sergeant added by way of explanation.

Callaghan looked up. 'The judge says there aren't the facilities to hold the trial here and he hasn't the time to travel. A deputy marshal will be arriving on the next stage from El Paso to take Gorman on to Tucson to be tried there.'

'Your people won't like it,' Pike warned him. 'Let's hope you don't have trouble.'

240

9

The death of Arthur Norris cast a sudden pall of gloom over the town. There was no longer any appetite for celebration, and Pike's men, though made welcome, felt that they were intruding on the people of Maxwell's grief. By noon they had saddled up and were ready to leave.

'You really don't have to go because of what's happened,' said Callaghan. 'At least stay on until tomorrow.'

'I've made one of my best men up to corporal. He'll take charge of them until they reach Fort Bowie, but I'll be staying on until that deputy marshal arrives.'

The sheriff looked puzzled. 'If they're going, there's no need for them to do so without you, although you're very welcome to stay.'

'You may not wanna hear this, Luke,

but when word gets around about the deal with Gorman you might have some trouble on your hands.'

'I know folks won't be happy, but this is a peaceful town. What are they going to do?'

'Come on, Luke. There's plenty o' folks ready to lynch a man if they get riled up enough. When a crime is committed someplace else, they want justice, but when one o' their own gets killed, they want revenge.'

Callaghan shook his head. 'I can't see that happening here.'

'Maybe not. I hope you're right but I'll stick around just in case.'

Pike's prediction appeared ominously correct as the day wore on. The mood darkened even further and groups of men gathered around outside the jail, muttering to each other.

'Come on, move along now, there's nothing to see here,' the sheriff admonished them.

'Nothin' to see except that little rat you got in there,' one of them, Abe

Gaston complained. 'You should let him hang here in front of us. How do we know some clever asshole lawyer won't get 'im off the charges in Tucson? It ain't no business o' that damned judge, anyhow!'

Abe was the town's blacksmith, a burly, unshaven individual given to drink and loud talk but usually harmless. Callaghan smelt whiskey on the man's breath as he met his belligerent, red-eyed gaze.

'He'll get a fair trial in Tucson the same as he would here, and there'll be all the same witnesses to give evidence against him. What difference does it make where he hangs?'

'I still say it ain't right, Sheriff. He killed Arthur right here in this town, and he oughta hang here! Now what are you gonna do about it!'

'I don't have the authority to go against a judge, Abe. You know that.'

Gaston favoured him with a sly grin. 'Yeah, but if he tried to escape, that'd be different. You'd have to shoot 'im down — only we might catch the varmint and hang 'im first!'

'Let me be clear. There'll be no fake escape and no lynching. Gorman will stand trial in Tucson like the judge ordered, and I'll do whatever it takes to uphold the law.'

Gaston grinned, showing his yellowed teeth. 'You can't do much if we all shove past you and . . . '

The blacksmith found himself staring down the barrel of Callaghan's revolver and the men who had gathered behind him fell back.

'Are you aimin' to use that thing?' asked Gaston, warily.

'You'll be the first to get a bullet and I'll take a few more out before the rest trample over me to reach Gorman's cell. Is it really worth that much to you?'

Gaston hesitated for a moment, then spat a stream of black juice from the tobacco he was chewing on to the ground. 'This'll be remembered come election time,' he warned. Then he and his companions sloped off.

'Next time there'll be more of 'em and they'll be prepared for trouble,' warned Pike, who had suddenly appeared at his elbow.

'It's turning out just like you said,' sighed Callaghan. 'I could do with a few of your men here to keep order.'

'Nah, you don't wanna do that. Soldiers are trained to kill, not to control angry civilians. Besides, the officers back at Fort Bowie wouldn't like it. Do you have a couple of good men you can trust?'

'Well, there's Matt Carver of course and a youngster called Mick Harper. He can be a bit of a hothead, but he fought well when we were attacked and he's a good kid, really.'

'If he can handle a rifle and take orders, the two of 'em should be enough. I got a few o' those new Winchesters and I reckon the four of us should hole up in the jail until the stage arrives. What do you say, Luke?'

Callaghan considered the sergeant's

suggestion for a moment. 'I don't have any better ideas. If folks try to get in, maybe a few warning shots will be enough to keep them at bay. I don't want to kill anyone if I can avoid it.'

'That's how I figured it. So, do you wanna get your friends, or shall I?'

'I'll go,' said Callaghan. 'I'll ask Matt to bring some food over. We'll need plenty of supplies if we're to last out until the stage gets here.'

Mick Harper did not need to be asked more than once and quickly began to close the hardware store he had inherited from his late uncle.

'You really don't have to do this, Mick. You've been in enough danger already.'

'It's OK, Sheriff. Uncle Linus was always tellin' me I should stand up for what was right, even when other folks wanted to go a different way. I didn't always listen then but I know what he'd want me to do.'

'He'd be real proud of you, I know that.'

The two men walked over to the way station and found Matt finishing off repairs to the roof which had been damaged during the battle with the Apaches. Callaghan called out for him to come down and he descended the ladder nimbly.

'What's up?' he asked.

The sheriff explained the situation and Pike's plan. 'We're not out of trouble yet, Matt. I could use your help, but I'll understand if you refuse. After all, you've got Rosie and Stevie to consider.'

'It won't be much of a town for them to live in if we don't keep order here.'

'Oh Lord, not more trouble!' Callaghan turned around to find Rosie standing behind him. 'At this rate, my husband will give up his business and sign on as your deputy,' she complained.

'I'm sorry to have to ask for more help but Matt's right. If we let people break in to the jail and lynch Gorman, we might as well all up sticks and move someplace else.'

'That's true, Ma'am. Uncle Linus used to say that the law stands between us and our worst instincts, so I reckon we gotta do like Sheriff Callaghan says,' Harper told her.

Rosie smiled and patted the young man on the cheek, much to his obvious embarrassment. 'You're getting just like old Linus yourself, God rest him.' Then she turned back to Callaghan. 'Well, you'll be needing some food if you're staying in that jail, I suppose.'

'Thanks, Rosie, that was my next request.'

'I'll get Christina to help me.'

The two women returned shortly afterwards with an enormous sack of provisions which they carried between them.

'I don't like this, Luke. Things could get very dangerous. If Gorman's going to hang anyway, why don't you just hand him over to them?'

'Like the way Gorman wanted us to just hand you over to Chico? Is this really any better?'

She looked down, her cheeks red with shame. 'I'm sorry, I shouldn't have said that.'

'I know you didn't mean it,' Callaghan replied as he placed his hand under her chin and lifted it gently upwards. 'You're just afraid, but it'll be all right, you'll see.'

'Can't I go in there with you? I can shoot as well as any man!'

The sheriff laughed. 'I know that. I've seen you do it, but there might not even be any shooting. Look, if you want to help, go find Samuel Endicott and get him to go around the town talking to people. Maybe he can calm things down and get them to see sense.'

Rosie put an arm around the younger woman's shoulders. 'Now that really could make a difference. Come with me and we'll go together.'

As the two women moved away, the three men made their way back to the jail. Pike was waiting for them and handed them each a rifle. Harper had not used a Winchester before and the sergeant went through the steps of how to load and fire one.

'If folks are comin' up close, why don't we just use pistols?' the younger man asked.

'Because these are louder and'll blow a bigger hole in a man at close range. What's more, folks know that and it makes 'em scared.'

Behind them, Gorman paced his cell nervously. 'You have to get me out of here, Sheriff. All I did was try to take some money which turned out to be fake, anyway. I don't deserve to get lynched for that.'

'People don't want to lynch you for stealing, you know that. Arthur Norris was a popular man in this town.'

'That was practically self-defence! His blood is on your hands, you know. You should never have sent him to spy on me like that.'

The former detective was sweating and stammering as he gripped the bars of the cell door. Callaghan looked at him in disgust and pointed the Winchester at his prisoner's chest.

'I swear to God, if you don't sit down and shut your lying mouth they won't have to lynch you because I'll blow a hole in you right now!'

'I think you should do what Sheriff Callaghan says,' added Harper helpfully.

As Gorman sat down on his bunk in despair, Pike stretched out a hand and gently lowered the barrel of the Winchester. 'Take it easy, Luke. I'm sure we're all tempted by that option, but we know it's not the right thing to do, you more than anybody.'

Callaghan nodded and rubbed a hand over his face. The strain of the past few days was beginning to tell on him. He turned back to the wretched man in the cell. 'I promise I won't shoot you unless you try to escape, but just try not to rile me, OK?'

Gorman nodded dumbly but said nothing further. Pike had told him about the plan to take him to Tucson and he hoped that he might be able to wriggle out of the worst charges if he could get clear of Maxwell. Jail was one thing, and hanging quite another, but to be lynched by a baying mob seemed the worst fate of all.

The next couple of hours passed quietly, but there was tension in the air. Eventually, Samuel Endicott passed by the window and Callaghan unbolted the door to let him in as the others stood guard.

'I'd like to be able to say that these precautions are unnecessary, Sheriff but I fear that would be a mistake.' The minister glanced at the men's rifles and sat down wearily.

'You've been around town then, Reverend?' Callaghan asked.

'Yes, I managed to persuade the majority to allow the law to run its course, but a few at least seem determined take the matter into their own hands.'

'Who are they?' asked Harper.

Endicott looked up at the younger

man and smiled. 'I'm glad to see you here, doing the right thing. To answer your question, Abe Gaston seems to be the ringleader. Bill Thornton, Nick Hoffman, Eugene Delmont and Curt Lazlo are ready to fight with him. There are a half dozen waverers I couldn't convince, weak men who'll wait to see what the others do.'

'What do you know about Gaston's friends?' asked Pike.

'Thornton owns the livery. Hoffman and Delmont both work for him. They're simple, uneducated men who know about horses and not much else. Arthur used to write letters for them to send to relatives so I guess they were pretty fond of him,' explained Carver.

'Lazlo's the town's apothecary. I'd expect him to have more sense,' added Callaghan.

'He's a professional man, it's true, but rather arrogant I'm afraid. Now, may I see the prisoner?' Endicott raised the bible he was carrying. 'His crimes may weigh heavily on him by now and he is surely in need of repentance.'

Callaghan jerked his head toward the cell door. 'Go ahead, Reverend, though I doubt it will do much good.'

The minister drew his chair up to the bars of the cell and engaged Gorman in a whispered conversation for several minutes. Callaghan motioned his companions to move to the other side of the room and they discussed what Endicott had told them.

'Even if all them who are minded to lynch Gorman turn up, there shouldn't be more than a dozen of 'em anyhow,' said Harper.

'That's still enough to cause a whole lotta trouble son, you'd better believe it,' Pike warned him.

'Yeah, but we'll fight 'em off, won't we?'

'Sure, Mick but it won't be easy. The question is, what exactly will they do?' asked Carver.

'It's getting dark now. My guess is they'll come at first light, make a lot of noise and demand we surrender

Gorman. When they don't get what they want, they'll start shooting at us and we'll have to shoot back.' Callaghan looked pointedly at Carver and Harper. 'These men are your neighbours, but if you hesitate we could end up getting killed.'

The station agent shrugged. 'I don't like it, but the law has to be upheld. Otherwise this town won't be worth a spit.'

'You can rely on me, Sheriff. I won't let you down,' the younger man added. 'Shouldn't we post a lookout though, just in case they do come tonight? I could take the first watch.'

Callaghan smiled at the young man's eagerness. 'OK, Mick, you do that.'

Behind them, Endicott intoned a brief prayer and then rose to leave. His expression was grim as he made for the door.

'I don't suppose you gotta confession, did you Reverend? It'd make things a whole lot easier,' Pike asked.

'No Sergeant. Mister Gorman will

only admit to being a thief, and he claims that even that is largely your fault.'

'Let's hope the jury in Tucson ain't taken in easy,' replied Pike gruffly.

'The truth will prevail, I'm certain of that.' The minister gave them a brief nod of farewell and stepped out into the orange glow of sunset. Callaghan hastily locked and bolted the door behind him. The world outside slowly dissolved into inky blackness as the four men watched the hours crawl by. They ate a pie Rosie had made, drank coffee and played cards. Even with Harper on watch, the others slept only fitfully. Eventually, Callaghan threw his blanket aside and went over to the window to take over.

'I was going to wake you in another hour, Sheriff.'

'It's OK, Mick. I wasn't asleep. Did you see anything?'

Harper squinted along the barrel of his Winchester. 'I thought I saw some lights a moment ago, figured I'd imagined it . . . No, wait . . . There it is again, look!'

Callaghan looked out of the window over his companion's shoulder and spotted the glowing flames of a torch-lit procession marching along the street. 'Come on, we've got company!' he called out to the others.

Carver and Pike were on their feet in an instant and took up positions with their rifles at the other windows. A terrified Gorman hid behind his bunk in a corner of the cell begging his guards to save him.

At last the group of men came to a halt and surrounded the jailhouse. Callaghan counted ten of them in the flickering torchlight. Abe Gaston stood at the front, flanked by Thornton and Lazlo. Thornton was a stocky individual with a bald head that looked as if it had been crammed between his shoulders. The apothecary was a tall, gaunt man with eyes that glinted coldly behind his spectacles. He made out Hoffman and Delmont standing just behind their boss, the former of slightly simian appearance with thinning, fair hair, while Delmont was darker with a sallow complexion.

'We don't want no trouble, Sheriff. Will you come out to parley? No man here's gonna shoot while we're talkin' and that's a promise!' Gaston's tone sounded conciliatory, despite the eerie atmosphere.

'All right, I'm coming out!' Callaghan replied.

'Are you crazy?' Carver seized his friend's arm. 'How do you know he won't shoot you down dead?'

'Gaston's a drunk and a hothead, but he's not a murderer. Maybe I can calm things down and make him see sense.'

'Luke's right. This could be our last chance to end this peacefully,' urged Pike.

Carver reluctantly stood aside as Callaghan opened the door, still armed with his rifle and stepped outside. Pointing the Winchester at Gaston's chest he told him to say his piece.

'That don't look too friendly,' the blacksmith admonished him.

The sheriff gestured with his weapon at the people gathered around. 'Neither does this, and I can see you're all armed. Now, what have you got to say?'

'We just want justice for Arthur, and the only way we can be sure 'bout gettin' it is if we see to it ourselves. Now, you just send Gorman out here and we'll do the rest. You don't have to play no part in it.'

A cheer went up from the small crowd and Thornton held up a coiled length of rope to indicate the seriousness of their intent. 'There's gonna be a hangin' here tonight!' he cried.

'Gorman will get a fair trial in Tucson, and then you'll get your hanging,' Callaghan replied. 'Look, I was there just after he killed Arthur. I'll testify to the fact that he shot an unarmed man who witnessed him stealing money. Pike will too. There's no chance he'll walk away from this.'

'If it ain't gonna make no difference,

anyway, why wait for a trial? Let's do it now!' cried Hoffman from the back.

'Because that's the law, it's what makes us civilized men instead of savages. Don't you see, the same law that protects Gorman from what you're trying to do is the same law that protects all of us from being lynched. Anyone can be accused of a crime, and if we stop using the law, the innocent will suffer along with the guilty.' A murmur ran through the crowd as some of them debated Callaghan's point.

'The point is, Sheriff, as you said yourself, this is a case in which there is no doubt about the man's guilt. All we want to do is make sure he's punished. If there was any doubt, we wouldn't have come, would we?' Lazlo smiled as he addressed this question to the men gathered behind him. They responded with shouts of approval.

Gaston spat out some tobacco juice on the ground. 'We've parlayed here long enough. Everybody's listened to what you gotta say and we've all been real respectful, you bein' our sheriff an' all. Now, are you gonna hand Gorman over or not?'

'I'm here to uphold the law and that's what I'll do,' Callaghan told them.

Delmont then waved his torch in the air. 'If we can't hang Gorman, we'll burn 'im out! What d'ya say folks?'

'Good idea, Eugene! We all got torches, Sheriff, and it'd be a lot easier to just do what we ask.'

'If you set fire to this building, the flames will spread and you could end up burning the whole town to the ground. How many would die then?'

'We all got guns too, Sheriff. There's more out here than you have in there,' Gaston told him.

'That's true,' conceded Callaghan. 'We could have a shootout here and now once I go back inside. But you'll have to put your torches out if you don't want to be spotted and gun fights in the dark are unreliable. Does anyone want to risk getting shot by his own side?'

Another murmur ran through the crowd and Gaston engaged in a hurried conversation with Lazlo.

'Very well, Sheriff. We'll all disperse to our homes for the time being, just to show that we want no unnecessary violence,' the apothecary announced. 'But we will return at first light and will expect our demand to be met.'

'Yeah, and we won't be comin' to talk, neither,' added Gaston before spitting a final stream of tobacco juice at the sheriff's feet.

The small crowd melted away into the night as Callaghan went back inside. 'That was close,' he told Pike as he sat down wearily.

'Words won't hold 'em off tomorrow,' the sergeant remarked. 'You'd better get some shut-eye. We need you shootin' straight when mornin' comes.' He turned to Harper. 'You too, young fella. I don't reckon we need to keep watch now the excitement's over with.'

The four men slept uneasily for the hours that remained until dawn. Gorman sat up on his bunk, waiting in terror for the first chink of light to appear in the sky.

'You won't be able to protect me. They'll hang me for sure!' Pale, wide-eyed and unshaven, the detective stared out at his captors through the bars of his cell.

'It's not you we're protecting, Gorman, it's the law and the reputation of this town,' Callaghan said roughly as he handed him a cup of steaming coffee. 'Drink, this. It'll calm your nerves.'

'I reckon that varmint'll die of fright afore anyone gets to put a goddamn rope around his neck,' commented Pike as he checked his rifle.

Carver was standing at the window watching the sun come up. 'Gaston and his friends are on their way,' he told them. He rammed the muzzle of his rifle against the window pane, shattering the glass and then thrust the barrel through the opening.

'Don't fire until they do,' warned the sheriff as he took up a position at the door and pulled up the blind. There was a square window in the central panel which he broke, and then stood to the side of it. Callaghan then gestured for Pike to stand in front of the window at the other side of him.

'Where do you want me, Sheriff?' asked Harper.

'Watch that window at the back. Some of them might come around that way,' Callaghan told him.

Gaston and his companions scattered as they approached the jailhouse, spreading themselves out to take up positions between buildings where they could find some cover. Callaghan spotted Thornton and Hoffman crouch down behind opposite ends of a water trough. Delmont dodged behind a bakery across the street from them, while Lazlo opened the door of a grain store a few doors down and slipped inside. A moment later, the muzzle of his rifle could be seen glinting in the early morning light. It looked like an old Henry that he had probably used during the war. Most were armed with pistols, however, probably Colts and Remingtons for the most part.

'This is your last chance, Callaghan, 'cos I'm through with talk. Are you gonna hand Gorman over or not?' The sheriff could hear Gaston loud and clear, but it was impossible to tell where he was hiding.

'I gave you my answer last night!'

There was a brief silence before the street echoed with the sound of gunfire. The shots came from all sides, splintering window frames and thudding into the walls of the building. The men inside fired back, Carver and Pike focusing on the pair shooting at them from the water trough. The combined firepower of their Winchesters blasted the roughly hewn planks apart until the structure almost collapsed, exposing the men behind it. Delmont tried to cover them from his hiding place across the street but Thornton was lifted off his feet as a bullet from Carver's rifle thudded into his chest. The pistol he had raised to fire before turning to run dropped from his dead hand as his body hit the ground. Hoffman was already running back across the street when he was cut down by a shot from Pike that hit him neatly between the shoulders.

The sight of his friends being gunned down in the street enraged Delmont and he rashly emerged from behind the bakery, firing shots from each of his two pistols.

'I'll kill all you goddamned bastards!' he screamed at them.

Callaghan's bullet went straight through the stable hand and he slumped against the wall of the bakery, leaving a long smear of blood behind him as his body slid to the floor.

The fighting continued but it was more sporadic now. Gaston's remaining men were well hidden but it was difficult for them to get shots in through the windows of the jailhouse. They had reached something of a stalemate and Callaghan wondered what Gaston would do to try and break it. The blacksmith had lost four men already without even injuring one of his opponents and was no closer to achieving his aim.

'Hey Callaghan! How about to a truce? It ain't dignified leavin' them dead folks lyin' like that in the street. Will yah hold your fire while we come out and get them poor souls?'

Callaghan looked questioningly at the others. 'It doesn't seem right to refuse a request like that.'

'No, but it could be a trap,' Carver warned him.

'Some goodwill might help bring this thing to an end,' suggested Harper from behind.

Pike shrugged. 'It could go either way, but it's your call.'

'All right, Gaston. Come out and get your dead!' Callaghan then watched nervously as the blacksmith and his followers crept out from their hiding places and picked up the bodies lying in the street. Then, out of the corner of his eye, the sheriff spotted a sudden movement as a figure darted across from the grain store and disappeared behind another row of buildings.

'You were right, Matt. Lazlo's trying to sneak around the back.' Callaghan then turned to Harper. 'Do you think you can handle it, Mick?'

The younger man grinned back at him. 'Sure, Sheriff. Just watch me!' With that, he opened the window at the back and then, to everyone's surprise, squeezed his agile frame through it and swung up on to the roof.

'What's that damn fool kid doin'? He's gonna get himself killed!' exclaimed Pike.

'I think he knows what he's up to. Let's just hope it works,' muttered Callaghan as he waited anxiously. Moments later they heard a loud thud when Harper landed on Lazlo as the apothecary reached his chosen spot.

There was a scuffling sound followed by a grunt.

'Hey, give us a hand here!' called out a familiar voice. Pike and Carver went to the back window and hauled an unconscious Lazlo through the opening. Harper then climbed back through, a triumphant smile on his face.

'You could easily have got killed there, Mick. Next time, just follow my orders, OK?' Callaghan admonished him.

The grin quickly faded. 'Yeah, but I did good, though, didn't I? I mean, now we got a hostage.'

'You're right, you did good. Just don't do it again,' the sheriff replied good-naturedly. He then went back to the front door. 'Hey, Gaston! Your little plan didn't work. We've got Lazlo in here!'

'It weren't nothin' to do with me! Whatever Lazlo did it was his own idea!' There was a tremor in the blacksmith's voice as he called back, a sure sign that he was lying, but

Callaghan let it pass.

'Well, if any more shots are fired, I'll throw him through this door and he can take his chances!'

'What do you want?' Gaston sounded hesitant and uncertain.

'Pull your men back. We'll keep Lazlo here until Gorman's on the stage tomorrow and then we'll release him!'

There was a long pause before the reply came. 'All right, Sheriff. You win for now!'

Callaghan watched as Gaston and his remaining companions crept off down the street, carrying their dead with them. He turned back to see that Lazlo was now slumped in a chair in handcuffs. The apothecary groaned and tried to stand as his consciousness returned but the sheriff pushed him back down firmly into his seat. It was going to be a long day.

10

'Hey, what's the idea? You can't keep me here!' protested Lazlo as he came to.

'Where you're concerned I can do any damn thing I want,' Callaghan told him. 'I could draw up a real long list of charges against you, including assault and attempted murder.'

'That's preposterous. I was merely doing my duty as a citizen.'

'Whether you like it or not, hanging a man without due process is murder. If any one of us in here had been killed during the attack, that would have been murder too, with you as an accessory.' The sheriff brought his face up close to Lazlo who now paled visibly and squirmed in his seat. 'In case you didn't know, that's a hanging offence.'

'Look . . . I just wanted to do right by Arthur Norris. You can't put me in the same category as him!' Lazlo raised his bound hands to point contemptuously at Gorman.

Carver shook his head. 'You just don't get it, do you? Electing yourself judge and jury makes you just as bad as he is.'

'We oughta throw you in that cell too,' added Pike.

'So, are you going to charge me with anything?' asked the chastened apothecary.

'Well, that depends. If you just sit there quietly and do what I tell you, maybe I'll forget about the charges,' Callaghan told him.

Lazlo nodded eagerly. 'OK, Sheriff. I'll do whatever you say.'

'Good. Now, there's just one problem left to solve. Matt, have you still got that old waggon you were storing behind the livery?'

'Sure I have. What do you want it for?' asked Carver.

'It's a long walk down the street from here to the stage,' explained Callaghan.

'We'll be pretty exposed and that's when Gaston and his friends will make their move.'

'Yeah, a high sided waggon with three of us ridin' shotgun could just give us the protection we'll need,' observed Pike. 'But how do we get it here?'

'I can go,' declared Harper.

'No, Mick, it's dangerous. You've done enough already,' Callaghan told him.

'I'm the only one who can get through that back window easily. I'm quick with horses, I can link up a team, drive it around the back and climb back in.'

Carver and Pike exchanged looks. 'It makes sense, and one of us has to go,' said the cavalry sergeant.

Callaghan nodded reluctantly. 'All right, Mick. You can go, but wait until dark.'

The hours of daylight crawled by as the men inside the jailhouse took turns on lookout, played cards and ate their meals. Their two prisoners remained quiet and gave them no trouble, Gorman having given up his whining. Maxwell was like a ghost town, since all those not taking part in Gaston's act of defiance had been warned firmly to remain in doors. Dusk came and went with no sign of an attack. Callaghan looked out and saw that the moon was almost full, riding high in an inky blackness speckled with stars.

'OK, kid. It's time to go.' He tossed Harper a rifle and told him not to be afraid to use it if necessary.

The young man nodded, gave them all a rueful smile and then squeezed his agile frame out through the back window before disappearing into the night. He crept softly through the back street that ran parallel to the main one until he reached the livery and slipped inside. The horses stirred in their stalls as he lit an oil lamp and held it up, selecting two of the strongest ones to pull the waggon. Sensing a movement behind him, he turned around, rifle at the ready.

'That don't look too friendly, Mick. I've known you since you came to live here.' Gaston stepped into the pool of lamplight, and as he emerged out of the shadows, Harper saw that he was swaying slightly. His left hand clutched a bottle of whisky, but a Colt revolver was firmly gripped in his right.

'That doesn't look too friendly either,' replied Harper.

'Oh, you don't wanna pay no mind to the fact that I'm holdin' a gun. I ain't got no wish to shoot you, Mick. You surely got no wish to shoot me, have you?'

Harper swallowed hard, recalling the blacksmith's past friendliness toward him. 'Just let me get these horses and the waggon out the back and I'll be gone.'

Gaston shook his head, still smiling. 'Can't let you do that, boy. You oughta be standin' by your friends, not helpin' that sheriff.' He reached out and placed a hand on the barrel of the rifle. 'Come on now, just put that down nice and easy, Mick.'

In one swift movement, Harper smashed the rifle against Gaston's right hand so that the gun dropped from his fingers. Then he lunged forward, sticking the muzzle into the older man's gut. The blacksmith sank to his knees with a choked cry and the boy then clubbed him over the head with the rifle butt so that Gaston was knocked out cold.

'You're right, I was never going to shoot,' remarked Harper to his friend's inert form and then quickly led the horses out of their stalls before hitching them to the waggon. The sound of hoofs and wheels clattering along the street sounded like a crescendo in his ears, but no one stirred as he sped back to the jailhouse and drew the waggon to a halt at the back.

'Did you have any trouble?' asked Callaghan as he helped Harper climb back in through the window.

'I had to knock out Abe Gaston. I guess he'll have a pretty sore head when he wakes up.'

'Maybe it'll knock some sense into him,' remarked Carver. 'At least you didn't have to shoot. Too many people have died over this already.'

'There might be more,' added Lazlo. 'Look, Sheriff, maybe I can help out. Let me go talk to the people involved. Perhaps I can persuade them to let things lie. After all, no one wants to be facing charges when all this is over.'

Callaghan considered this for a moment. 'No, right now you being here is probably the one thing that stops Gaston's friends from attacking us. I'm not about to give that up. If you want to help, just sit tight and wait until morning. I'll tell you what I want you to do then.'

'Will those horses be all right out there?' asked Pike, changing the subject.

'Yeah, I brought some feed and blankets for them, and we've got enough water,' Harper told him.

The sergeant nodded approvingly. 'I could make a good soldier outta you.

The rule is that the horses get looked after first, then the men, and yourself last.'

Another night of tense, uneasy sleep followed before the hours of daylight crept toward noon, Callaghan anxiously checking his pocket watch every five minutes. At last it was almost time for the stage to arrive.

'Ten minutes to go. Mick, you can get that waggon and bring it around to the front now.'

As Harper climbed back through the back window once more, the sheriff unlocked Gorman's cell and gestured for the prisoner to come out. The disgraced detective shuffled forward reluctantly.

'Come on, hurry it up. The only alternative to getting on that stage is to get lynched here. What's it going to be?'

As Gorman emerged, Callaghan shoved him in Pike's direction. 'OK, guard him for me, would you?'

Carver opened the door a crack as the waggon drew up outside. Callaghan told him to go in front, rifle at the ready, then Gorman with Pike taking up the rear.

'You still haven't said what you want me to do,' said Lazlo nervously.

The lawman then hauled him to his feet and slid the barrel of a rifle between the hostage's cuffed wrists, the muzzle resting under Lazlo's chin.

'I want you to stand alongside me on that waggon for everyone to see. I hope your friends value your life, because if one of them tries anything I'll blow your damned head off. Is that clear?'

The apothecary gave a slight nod, his eyes wide with terror, and then the group emerged into the midday sunshine. Carver leaped up beside Harper to ride shotgun and Pike followed, pushing Gorman up on to the waggon in front of him. It was difficult keeping the rifle in position while clambering up on to the vehicle with his hostage, but Callaghan managed it. The two then remained standing as the waggon moved off, the lawman urging Harper to drive slowly.

The street was deserted, the shutters closed at every window, although one or two of them opened a crack so that the curious could take a peep at what was going on. Callaghan held the rifle under Lazlo's chin with his left hand, a revolver gripped in his right. His eyes scanned the street ahead, glancing up at the rooftops for signs of movement but so far there was nothing. At last the way station came within sight and Callaghan could see the stage approaching in a cloud of dust. It was going to be right on time. Between them and it, however, Gaston stood flanked by two confederates. The sheriff guessed they were the only men he had left. The blacksmith looked a sorry sight with a bloodstained bandage wrapped around his head, but he held his rifle straight and it was pointed at Callaghan.

'That's as far as you go, Sheriff. Gorman ain't gettin' on that stage.'

Callaghan lowered the rifle slightly as the waggon drew to a halt. 'For God's sake, Abe, back off! He'll kill me if you don't!' pleaded Lazlo.

Gaston hesitated for a moment and his two men looked uncertain. 'Sheriff Callaghan here's a real upstandin' lawman. He won't do no such thing, so don't you fret none.'

'Are you sure you want to take that risk?' the lawman asked.

Gaston nodded. 'I'm sure. Now, y'all got rifles and so have we. Either it gets nasty or you hand Gorman over. What's it gonna be?'

Callaghan sighed. 'You're right, Abe. I can't shoot this unarmed man and I don't want to risk getting gunned down in the street.' He threw his rifle aside and shoved Lazlo down from the waggon. Gaston grinned and visibly relaxed as he and his companions lowered their weapons. In that split second the lawman moved in an arc, firing his pistol at each man in turn with incredible swiftness. The one to Gaston's right crumpled as a bullet hit him straight through the heart, the blacksmith got one between the eyes and the third man fell with a choked cry as the next shot ripped through his carotid artery.

'My God, I ain't never seen anything like it,' muttered an amazed Pike.

'I hope you never have to see it again,' said Callaghan ruefully as he holstered his weapon. 'Well, the show's over so let's get Gorman on that stage.'

The weary passengers tumbled out to stretch their legs for a few moments when the Concord coach drew to a halt. The last to emerge was a heavyset man with mutton-chop whiskers who wore a deputy marshal's badge pinned to his cowhide waistcoat.

'I believe you're here to collect this man,' said Callaghan as he shoved Gorman toward him.

The deputy glanced at the dead men lying in the street. 'I see you had a little trouble, Sheriff. Friends of his, were they?'

There was a moment's pause before Callaghan and his companions burst into uncontrolled fits of laughter. The deputy shook his head in puzzlement, then bundled his prisoner aboard the stage. A quick change of horses followed and then the three men watched as the stage grew smaller and then faded into the distance, leaving only dust behind it.

As Callaghan turned around, Lazlo appeared at his elbow. 'I wonder if you'd mind removing these,' he said, raising his cuffed wrists.

'Sure, you're free to go now,' said the lawman as he unlocked the cuffs.

'Were you really prepared to shoot me?'

'What do you think?'

'It does seem rather strange, considering how important you think it is to uphold the law.'

Callaghan nodded. 'Exactly. That's why the rifle I was holding had no bullets in it.'

Lazlo thought about this for a moment. 'I guess you wanted to give Gaston and his friends a good reason to give up.'

'You're right. I figured there'd been enough killing, but you can't convince some people.'

The apothecary looked down at the dirt. 'I realize now how wrong I was to get involved. I'm sorry for all the trouble.'

'Well, you didn't start it. Abe Gaston did, and now he's paid with his life. I guess that'll be a lesson to you.'

'It certainly will.' Lazlo extended his hand and the sheriff shook it as the two men parted.

The town was starting to get back to normal now that the drama was over. The corpses of Gaston and his men were removed from the street. Shutters were opened, and people started to come out of their houses.

Callaghan heard a shout of joy and turned to see Christina running down the street toward him. Moments later, they were embracing as townspeople gathered around the happily reunited couple.

'Well, I guess I'd better get back to

Fort Bowie and leave you lovebirds to it,' declared Pike.

'Oh no you don't!' Christina admonished him as she broke away from kissing the sheriff. 'We're going to have the best wedding ever. You must stay for that.'

'Hey, aren't I supposed to ask you a question first?'

'Why do you need to ask when you already know the answer?'

Callaghan shrugged. 'I guess not.' Then he kissed her again, and this time there were no interruptions.

THE DEFENDERS

Alex Hawksville

Ex-bounty hunter Jubal Thorne wants nothing more than to settle down to a peaceful life when he rides into Brewlins, Wyoming. What he gets is something else entirely. Caught up in a bidding wrangle for a local ranch with Abbey Watt, he buys the land and she buys the steers. But trouble is brewing with powerful cattleman Chas Stryker, who wants the spread for himself. When Thorne finds the former owner of his ranch shot dead in his own house, he knows he'll be defending his claim with his six-gun . . .

THE HOMESTEADER'S WAR

Doug Bluth

Former Union solder and Colorado rancher Ned Bracken wants nothing more than to enjoy a quiet life with his family. Instead, he's hounded by representatives from the railroad who want him to sell his land. When raiders burn his ranch and kidnap his wife, Ned is pushed too far. Now he's out for blood, and determined to find his beloved wife, Betsy. In a race against time, Ned must battle outlaws, tie-down artists, and ghost from his past to rescue her — and to redeem himself in his own personal war.

BLACK HILLS GOLD

Will DuRey

Since the signing of the Laramie Treaty, the tribes of the Plains have practised their nomadic lifestyle within the boundaries of the lands set aside for their use. While the Americans, the *wasicun*, stay away, the tenuous peace is maintained. One word, however, uttered at a riverside meeting with Yellowstone Kelly raises Wes Gray's concern that white men might soon breach the borders of the Great Sioux Reservation and bring with them the turmoil of war. The object of their trespass? To gain that for which men will risk all: gold.

EVEN MARSHALLS HANG

Sam Clancy

When it comes to fighting outlaws, Josh Ford, Deputy United States Marshal, is hell on wheels — and this time he'll need to be. Two other lawmen have disappeared in the Moose River Mountains, and the trail leads to Stay, a small town under the heel of a brutal vigilance committee led by a killer known only as The Judge. After Ford is forced into a gunfight he doesn't want, and then sentenced to hang, the stench of death only gets stronger. They were warned. They've never seen the likes of Ford!